The
Road
to
Easton

by
Jordan Richbourg

THE ROAD TO EASTON

ISBN-13: 978-1098651374

Author: Jordan Richbourg

Edited by David S. Larson

Cover design by Kari Cureton

DEDICATION

To my wife, Christina, who was my light
in the darkest days of my life.

To Beau and Ryan for believing in me
when it was so easy to forget who I was.

Without these three,
this book would not be possible.

To everyone out there facing dark times
and making hard choices,
what is meant to be will find its way.

The two most important days in your life are the day you are born and the day you find out why.

Mark Twain

1

RYAN

R yan Turner blinked open his eyes, loud voices waking him from a sweet dream. He gave a groggy stretch and looked at his clock.

"Eleven twenty-three on a Sunday," he grumbled as he rubbed his face awake.

He threw off his blanket and pulled down his worn Kalamazoo High Hornet's football jersey that had scrunched up while he slept. He rolled out of bed and stood, staring at the weathered American Flag in the window, blocking out most of the sun's rays.

He shook his head clear, dropped and completed 50 pushups—back flat as a board, chest just touching the worn gray carpet with each rep—his twice-daily routine. Breathing hard, he opened his bedroom door, the sweet scent of deer sausage greeting him. Mixed with it was the familiar tension of an argument brewing between his parents. There was no stopping sound with the paper-thin walls in their double-wide manufactured home. He paused.

"But why did you cash in our life insurance without talking to me, Alvin?"

She used "Alvin"—oh, boy, Ryan thought.

1

Ryan's father responded in a calm, apologetic tone, "Honey, I did it for Ryan. He's our only child. Eastern Michigan is over ten grand a year, and more with him renting an apartment. The insurance policy only covers half. We need to make up the rest."

He heard the sausages sizzle as his mother pushed them around in the pan. Other than that, silence.

His father started up again. "He's waited two years, Kathy. Besides, he needs to get away from Mendon. This isn't a place for a young man like Ryan with all his potential and dreams. This town is where dreams come to die."

She sniffled. "I know."

His voice softened. "I'm hoping you can pick up more hours up at the salon."

She sighed. "You're right. Eastern Michigan is a good school." It was both a question and a hopeful statement. "But what if something happens? We don't have insurance." Her worry punctuated every word.

"We're in good health, Kathy. I cut back on more than the life insurance—took out a second on this place, and put off buying a new truck. Everything's been put on hold until I land a new job and we sort it all out."

Ryan stomped his feet and cleared his throat on the way into the kitchen. "Good morning," he said cheerfully.

His mother turned away and wiped her face with her apron. His father stood by their yellow Formica dinette table, his grease-stained bib overalls hiding most of a worn green Army jacket with "TURNER" above the pocket. The newspaper lay unopened—unlike him.

"Everything okay?" he asked.

"Sure," his mother said and whirled around with two plates brimming with hash browns, scrambled eggs, and sausage. "You best eat now." She nodded her head for Ryan and Alvin to sit, then poured them coffee.

She ate by the stove as usual, her face filled with the simple satisfaction of feeding her men hearty food—but with an underlying worry. Change was coming.

Ryan sprinkled tabasco on his plate and dug in, but the silence kept getting in the way of him enjoying his meal. "Hey, Dad, you gonna work on the truck today?"

His father answered, "Work *on* it? Give me some credit, college boy. I work *under* that old Chevy on the tranny."

They both chuckled and the tension ended, like breaking loose a stubborn bolt on a rusted engine.

"So, I was thinking—maybe after your mother and I come back from your aunt's, we can get in some fishing on Morrow Lake. You know, before your first day of college and all?"

Ryan sat up and leaned forward. The thought of doing anything outdoors excited him. "You sure? I don't want to get in the way of anything, like..." his voice trailed off. Ever since his father lost his job six weeks ago, all he'd been doing was looking for work.

"All's well, Son."

"Well then, yeah, I'm in!"

His mother cleared her throat.

His father turned to her. "It's one day, Kathy. Heck, it's one afternoon. No one's gonna want to interview me on a Sunday, for God's sake."

3

His mother dumped her empty plate and fork into the sink—extra loud for emphasis.

His father ignored her. "You can tell me all about this new degree you're gonna get. I know you thought about the military while you were working and saving for school—but that's a last option. It changes a man—I should know." He patted his right thigh where a Viet Cong grenade took half the muscle. He never wore shorts.

"You got it." Ryan excused himself and went to his room, put in his ear buds and turned up the volume. He opened the Eastern Michigan University catalog, its pages worn from overuse, like the *Playboys* he used to hide under his mattress. He drooled over pictures of the student gym, not able to afford even a YMCA membership.

The new parks and recreation major was why he chose EMU. His love of the woods and water began at an early age, his father taking him camping and fishing—years in the Boy Scouts multiplying those feelings. There was something pure and honest about being alone in the woods.

"The elements are the best way to test what kind of man you are," his father always said.

He didn't understand those words when he was young, but they made sense now. Ryan was his father's son in appearance—tall with blond hair, though his eyes came from his mother, a soft shade of olive green.

"Hard work will make you a hard man," his father told him repeatedly. Alvin Turner was a welder by trade, but fusing molten metal together at 3,500 degrees was not what made him hard—it was the war.

Ryan worked construction the past two summers, but didn't feel he measured up in toughness to his father—a granite boulder of a man, and impossible to read.

A loud knock on Ryan's bedroom door had him turn around and take out his ear buds.

His father poked his head in. "We're heading out, going through some of your Uncle's old things. We'll get back around four-thirty." His face lit up. "Hit the lake then?" he asked.

Ryan smiled and nodded his head. "Perfect."

After his father left, he popped his ear buds in again, and sorted through the books.

Do good. They're counting on you.

He picked up "English 101: First-Year Composition" and opened to the first page.

***

A loud knock on the door startled Ryan awake and he sat up in bed. Text books were scattered all over his comforter along with the latest issue of *Backpacker Magazine*. His mother poked her head in the door.

"We're back. Mind if I come in?" She smiled with a warmth Ryan hadn't seen in a long time.

"Sure."

He stacked the books and she sat on the bed, straightening his worn comforter. She looked as if she wanted to say something, but had trouble finding the words.

"Hey, Mom," Ryan said softly and reached out to touch her hand.

"I'm so proud of you, Ryan. I want you to know that." She reached for a picture frame on his night stand.

"I know."

She gazed at his high-school football picture with tears in her eyes. "You're going to do so well in school." She put the photo back and kissed the top of his head like she did ever since he was a kid. "You'll be the first Turner to go to college. Your father and I, well, we started school, but life kind of got in the way. And then you were born. Not that you weren't the best thing that could have happened to us. We didn't even think we could have children."

Ryan cocked his head to the side and crinkled his forehead. "Really?"

"Yes. Doctors told us, what with your father's war injury and all, we shouldn't count on it—but then, well, there you were. I don't know how on God's green earth we raised such a fine young man, but I wouldn't trade a minute of it for the world." Tears welled in her eyes and she sniffed. "Now, you best get along—your father's waiting on you, and so are the fish."

***

It was almost six o'clock before they launched their 14-foot aluminum outboard onto Morrow Lake, a light breeze leaving the water as a still mirror, and a full moon peeking over the horizon with nearly two hours of daylight remaining.

His father let Ryan steer the boat out to their favorite spot. "Shut off the engine now and let's drift the next fifty feet—don't want to disturb the catfish."

Quietly they went about baiting their hooks and casting their lines like they did hundreds of times before—but somehow this time was different. They both knew that after today, things would never be the same.

They took in the late afternoon's sounds of water slapping against the hull and occasional egrets croaking as they skimmed the water looking for a meal. The warmth and humidity of the early September evening brought out the fireflies who lit up the trees and bushes with their pulsing dance.

After twenty minutes, Al pulled in a fat 18-incher. "Guess who's got some catching up to do?" They both laughed, knowing he somehow always caught the first fish.

After taking out the hook and putting the fish in the creel, Alvin paused. "Ryan, I want you to know something." He cleared his throat before he continued. "I raised you to be the man I never was."

It was unlike his father to show emotion. Ryan whispered, "Dad."

"Your mother, she taught me to love again after the war, and you're a direct creation of our love for each other. I love you, Ryan." Alvin reached out and patted his son's shoulder.

"Me too, Dad."

Ryan's line jerked and it snapped them out of the moment. "Look who's got one now."

They made it back to shore hours later with seven catfish and grins that wouldn't stop. After they loaded the boat onto the trailer and hopped in the truck, Alvin paused before starting the ignition. He looked to Ryan. "It was really something out there today, wasn't it?"

"Yes, it was, Dad. It really was."

***

Ryan's alarm was set for seven a.m., but he was up an hour early. *First day of college.* He bounced out of bed and immediately counted out 50 perfect pushups. While he waited for the shower to warm up, he brushed his teeth and shaved. After the shower, he wrapped a towel around his waist and darted down the hall, ducking into his room.

Blue jeans, plaid green shirt, lace-up brown boots, and a Gor-Tex jacket—he was ready, except—he glanced around. There on the back of the door was a worn Detroit Tigers hat. He'd already packed his car the day before, hardly room for anything else. He donned the cap, nodded into the mirror with confidence, grabbed his backpack, and headed out of his room.

His mother caught Ryan mid-stride as he opened the front door. "You need good food to study hard." She handed him a brown lunch bag, then kissed him on the cheek.

He left a "Thanks, Mom" hanging in the air as he bolted out the door.

***

Two hours later he pulled his 1990 faded green Ford Escort into the freshman parking lot of Eastern Michigan University. He felt old at twenty as a freshman, but those two years of working construction gave him extra initiative to study and do well. With 21,000 students, he wasn't going to stand out, that's for sure.

He found his English class and took a seat in a lecture hall that held 200 students. There was a buzz of excitement—so different from high school where everyone tried to ditch classes and were in their cliques, jockeying to be noticed. The professor looked 50ish with glasses and a graying goatee. He talked so fast, Ryan worked hard to keep up, scribbling in a new notebook. The other students used tablets and laptops to either record the lecture or take notes.

With a one-hour break between subjects, he slung his backpack over his shoulder and went looking for the dining hall to eat whatever his mother packed him.

You're right, Mom, studying makes me hungry.

"Hey, Turner!" someone yelled from behind him.

Ryan turned around but couldn't find the voice in the sea of students.

"Turner!" the voice yelled again. "I know you hear me."

Ryan pressed himself against the wall, and on his tiptoes spotted Brock Peterson, a huge defensive lineman who played on the Kalamazoo High football team.

"Brock, I didn't think you could get any bigger," Ryan said giving Brock a fist bump.

"Tipping two-eighty now. Protein, man, and lots of weight training." He poked Ryan in the shoulder with his big paw. "So, the star quarterback finally going to school?" He looked around then leaned in. "We could use you."

"Not this year—gotta get good grades. Maybe I could do the walk-on thing next year if I juice up and work out like you. Not everyone gets a scholarship." Ryan poked him back.

"Two more years and I'm going pro—defensive end. I can feel it!" He looked down at his phone. "Shit, gotta get to class." He walked away but yelled over the heads of students as he sped down the hall. "Listen, I got the same number. We can hit some parties this weekend, since you're a freshman and all." Brock's smile faded into the throng of students.

"Yeah, man. That'd be great," Ryan said into the air.

***

The entire week was a blur, Ryan's notebook brimming with notes and his head swimming with all the assignments he needed to complete. He smiled the entire way home, not caring how heavy the traffic was, his mind overflowing with everything—the campus—the classes—the students—the cute coeds. It was happening and better than he expected, way better. He called his father to let him know he was going to be late, but only got voicemail. The same thing with his mother. *Hmm.*

His car sputtered as he pulled into the uneven gravel driveway just as the sun set around eight o'clock. He hopped out, anxious to share his first week in college with his parents—they sacrificed so much to get him there.

He picked up the mail and was lost in reading a notice from his college, crossing the wooden deck he and his father built the year before. In a fog, he reached for the doorknob, but it wasn't there. The front door was wide open.

Huh?

Ryan shuffled inside cautiously and switched on the lights. The living room was a mess, furniture turned over and bookshelves empty, their contents on the carpet. He stepped on a family picture that belonged on an end table, cracking it even more. He picked it up and laid it on the table. It wasn't cold, but a shiver went through him.

"Hello?" he called out.

Nothing. Silence.

"Hey, Mom? Dad?"

Ryan took out his phone and called his father, his heart thumping in his chest as he looked around. A faint ringtone came from the kitchen and he followed it. He flicked on the lights and looked down—stepping back as if that could erase the memory. "No…" his voice trailed off.

His father's voice came out of Ryan's phone. "You've reached Alvin Turner. I'm unavailable right now. If you leave…"

Ryan couldn't listen anymore and stumbled out the front door. He leaned over and wretched, his body revolting from the bloody images. His hands trembled as he dialed 9-1-1.

"Nine-one-one dispatch. State your name and emergency please."

"Ryan, Ryan Turner," he gasped.

"Mr. Turner? State your emergency please."

He froze, looking back to the front door, trying to wrap his mind around the horror he witnessed.

"Please state your emergency, Ryan," she repeated.

"My, my parents have been … I think they're dead," he whispered.

2

RYAN

Scattered across Ryan's small front yard were six idling squad cars. Their spinning blue and red lights cast an eerie glow off the fall leaves high above the manufactured home complex. Occasionally, a police radio cut through the night, other than that, the only sound was the throaty drone from the engines of the police cars, like a distant storm approaching.

Neighbors came of out of their houses and stood in small clusters pointing and whispering, some speaking with officers. Yellow crime scene tape formed a twenty-foot radius around Ryan's home. The medical examiner's van arrived and backed into the driveway boxing in Ryan's car. The driver and his assistant exited and went around to open the back double doors, pulling out two gurneys.

Ryan sat in the passenger seat of a cruiser next to a detective taking notes. Ryan glanced over at the gaping front door of his home and shuddered at the sight of two gurneys being wheeled in.

"I think that's all for now, Mr. Turner," Detective Washburn said closing his note pad.

Mr. Turner. That's my father's name—was *my father's name.*

Ryan's head involuntarily twitched, his breath still in shallow gasps ever since he came home.

Washburn handed Ryan his card. "We'll want you down at the station Monday, in the afternoon, say two o'clock? Sometimes after a few nights' sleep you'll recall something that can be of help. The address is on my card."

Ryan looked down at the card. "Okay, Detective Washburn," he whispered.

"Again, I'm sorry for your loss." Washburn reached over and placed his hand on Ryan's shoulder, letting it rest there like his father Alvin often did.

***

Ryan spent a fitful night in his car in the Walmart parking lot, the thought of crossing the threshold into his parents' home too much for him. While he washed up in the store's restroom in the morning, his phone rang. He looked at the caller ID.

Aunt Morgan—I should've called.

"Hello," Ryan answered.

"Oh, my god, Ryan," her voice trembled. "My poor brother Alvin, and Kathy…" she trailed off.

"I know. I—I found them." The images flashed through his mind again—he gulped air.

"Did you … where did you spend the night?"

"In my car."

She sniffled. "Well, you'll be staying with me from now on, and I won't take no for an answer."

***

The next two days were filled with phone calls from friends and relatives, some Ryan never met. "We're so sorry." "You know Alvin was my favorite cousin." Sympathy for their loss—not Ryan's. He was glad when his cell phone battery finally died Sunday afternoon. Aunt Morgan was aware of his grief and gave him distance as he struggled with his deep loss.

When Ryan woke early Monday, his first thought was to start the long drive to Eastern Michigan University—but it would have to wait while he sorted things out. He looked at his backpack filled with books, his notes, and assignments from what seemed a lifetime ago. Before he left the house, he scribbled a note to Aunt Morgan. "Got a few errands to run. See you around noon."

He drove by Kalamazoo Central High and parked, the campus bustling with the start of a new football season. Some of his best memories were on this field, taking the Maroon Giants to the state title in his senior year as quarterback.

Chelsea Wilkinson. I wonder what happened to her.

She was his girlfriend the last three years of high school, then she headed to Michigan State on a cheerleading scholarship. It had been two years since he saw her, promising to stay in touch after graduation. Once she started at State though, it went from talking every day to a few times a week, then once a week—then it was over. There weren't any tears, but there were unfinished hearts.

He dozed off and was jolted awake when a security guard tapped on his car window.

"Huh?" he said groggily.

"You're not allowed to park here during school hours," the security guard said pointing to a sign.

Ryan nodded, started up his car, and aimlessly drove back streets until he found himself in front of his home. The yellow crime scene tape was still strung between the trees, a reminder to everyone that a horrible crime happened here. He waited an hour, trying to find the courage to cross the threshold again. All he wanted to grab was a few pictures, a trophy or two, or an heirloom that held deep memories that would be impossible to fade. He put his hand on the door handle and froze.

I can't.

He got to his Aunt's home to find a sandwich on the kitchen table along with a note saying she was at the grocery store.

He was tempted to turn on the TV to drone out the dull static in his head, but was sure they'd keep mentioning his parents' murder. The average number of murders for Kalamazoo was eight a year—a fact Detective Washburn shared. It was almost as if to say that his parents were now a statistic, no longer Alvin and Kathy Turner.

He finished eating and went to his room, sitting on his bed, knees folded up to his chin while he waited to leave for his appointment at the police station.

Just before two p.m., Ryan parked and then walked toward the front glass doors of the Kalamazoo Police Station. The brick building was framed with neatly-placed shrubs, a well-kept lawn, and lush poplar trees—not at all how Ryan felt, so chaotic. He stepped inside and approached the visitor's desk, a uniformed female officer greeting him. He asked for Detective Washburn and was told to take a seat.

Ryan didn't have to wait but a few minutes before Washburn showed up, a manila file folder in his hand. The detective looked different from Friday night when he sat across from Ryan in the front seat of a police cruiser. He was shorter and had a hardness to him.

You didn't get much sleep either, did you?

"This shouldn't take long." They shook hands.

Washburn looked Ryan in the eye, a feeling of dread hitting Ryan.

The detective cocked his head and said, "Follow me."

Washburn led Ryan into a small room where they took seats across from each other at a gray metal table. Washburn opened the file and went over the details of his interview from Friday night, noting minor additions or changes Ryan suggested.

"Well, that's about it," Washburn said and went to stand.

Ryan didn't budge. "Who … who did this?" he asked through clenched teeth.

Washburn sat back down. "We don't know—yet. We finished gathering the forensics, now begins our analysis of all the materials. That reminds me, we need to get your prints."

Ryan wrinkled his brow.

"We dusted for prints everywhere. We have your parents, and once we add yours, we'll hopefully find fingerprints that don't match. We'll compare those in our database and find who did this. It's most likely a career criminal with a record. With no witnesses, that's what we got going so far."

Washburn tapped his pen on the folder signaling to Ryan the detective wanted to tell him more, but wasn't sure.

"What else?" Ryan asked.

Washburn cleared his throat. "The coroner's preliminary report indicates your parents' death occurred late Thursday night or early Friday morning."

The thought of his parents lying on the kitchen floor for almost a day, caused Ryan to catch his breath and turn pale.

"You okay?" Washburn asked and stretched his arm across the table to touch Ryan's shoulder.

Ryan nodded. "When you say death, don't you mean murder?"

"Yes." The detective pulled his hand back. "We'll contact you if anything changes. Now to get you printed." He stood again and held out his hand.

Ryan left the station 10 minutes later, working to rub off gunk from the fingerprinting, still hidden in the creases of his fingers. Ryan sat in his car, wondering what to do next, when his phone rang—an unknown caller. He hesitated, then tentatively answered, "This is Ryan Turner."

"Mr. Turner, we heard about your loss and wish to express our deepest condolences."

"Who is this?"

"I'm Paul Wagner from Pearson Mortuary. I wonder if I might have—"

Ryan hung up and stared at the phone, a headache starting. *How'd you get my number?*

***

When he got home and went into the kitchen, Aunt Morgan was there with her ever-present blue apron, hovering over the stove, stirring something. She let her hair go gray years before and piled it on top of her head, wearing the frumpy look of a lifelong widow. Her smile was her best feature, and she gave it freely.

She turned to Ryan, "Set two places, will you? It's mac and cheese night."

Over dinner, the discussion they needed to have finally took root. "I got a call from a mortuary today," Ryan said.

"Yes, I guess we've got some planning to do." Aunt Morgan reached over and patted Ryan's arm. "We'll figure this out. You don't have to do it all on your own."

"I don't even know where to start." Ryan pushed his plate aside.

"Well, it's been forty-five years since your uncle John passed, and the military managed most of that. I'll make some calls tomorrow. You ought to get to bed."

Ryan shuffled off to his room and collapsed on his bed, too tired to clean up, and fell into a dark sleep.

***

The two-hour drive from Kalamazoo to Eastern Michigan University was long and lonely—Ryan didn't even turn on the radio for company. The admissions office shared their sympathy, but weren't able to refund the full amount of his tuition, Ryan leaving with their promise to send him a $1,100 check in a few weeks. The bookstore was worse, claiming his books were used. No amount of pleading helped, and he ended up getting only $250 from the $700 he paid.

He left the bookstore, crossing the quad slowly, taking one last look at his future as it slipped past. Someone tapped him on the shoulder and he spun around to find Brock Peterson.

"Sorry, man—I heard about your folks and all." Brock tried to give a brave smile and they shared a weak fist bump.

"Yeah, I was just at admin." Ryan look down and shuffled his feet.

"You aren't dropping out, are you?"

"Got to. Need the money. Heart's not in it, then there's the funeral and stuff."

"Oh, man. Bummer. Well, I'll try to make the funeral. You got brothers and sisters?"

"No. I'm the only Turner left." Those words lodged in Ryan's throat and he had to look away. "Hey, I gotta get going." He turned back to find Brock's mouth open, not knowing what to say. "I'll catch ya later, Brock."

"Sure."

Ryan couldn't get to his car fast enough. He looked back at the bustling campus, then drove the six blocks to his apartment. He packed his car in half an hour, left a note for the landlord, keys for his roommates, and drove away.

The two-hour drive to Kalamazoo was a blur of tears that wouldn't stop, Ryan's sleeves soaked by the time he pulled into Aunt Morgan's home. Two stories, cream-colored with faded blue shutters, a brick front porch—a worn-out 60s tract home waiting for care. Aunt Morgan's car wasn't in the driveway, so he wouldn't have to explain his puffy eyes to her.

***

Wednesday morning Ryan woke to a knock on his bedroom door. "Ryan, may I come in?" Aunt Morgan called through the door.

"Sure," Ryan said as he rubbed his face awake.

She stepped in, careful not to disturb the piles of clothes Ryan stacked on the floor. She stood at the foot of his bed. "Oh, they're from my apartment. I'll put 'em away today." He put on his best smile.

"I spoke to the pastor over at First Baptist, you know, where your folks went to church sometimes. Well, they'd like to help with the memorial and funeral, which is going to be a blessing, but still it's going to cost ten thousand dollars or so." She took a few loose strands of her gray hair and tried to get them to join the others on top of her head. "I don't really have any savings..." her voice drifted off.

"My folks cashed in their life insurance so I could go to school. I've got fourteen hundred or so coming—from admissions and books." He gauged her caring wrinkled brow. "I had to drop out of EMU—for now." The loss of his future hit him again, he caught his breath, and steadied himself with a fragment of hope. "I can get a grand for Dad's truck, and maybe eight hundred for the boat."

She sat on the edge of his bed and picked at the edges of the worn floral comforter, her head downcast. "You're the only family I have left. Like I said, we'll figure something out." She looked up with moist eyes that matched Ryan's.

***

The funeral was quiet and simple, but Ryan's few words had to be pulled from his throat. What he said couldn't come close to what his parents meant to him. Aunt Morgan and Ryan shook the hands of 70 or so well-wishers and took their half-hugs, people who didn't want to come too close to death.

It surprised Ryan that Detective Washburn showed up, the last in the receiving line. "Sorry for your loss." He looked around to make sure no one was within earshot and leaned in. "Come by the station when you can. I believe we have a break in your case."

***

Detective Washburn leaned forward and opened a file folder. "We have a positive ID on the killer. We ran DNA tests and matched them to a man with a history of burglary, small-time theft, and assault. He's one of those off-the-grid types."

Ryan sat up in his chair and gulped.

"His name's Russell Stevens." Detective Washburn continued as he reached inside the folder and pulled out a large mugshot. "The guy's been arrested on small crimes over the past twenty years and in five states, spending lots of time in and out of jail. I'm not going to lie to you, this is the biggest crime he's ever committed. He'll be tough to catch, but we'll get him. These kinda guys always screws up."

Ryan stared at the mugshot—a wild-haired burly man, almost like a lumberjack, with dark uncaring eyes. The crime scene surged into his mind—his parents on their backs on the kitchen floor, his mother's dress pulled up, her panties around her knees, a large knife sticking out of his father's chest. Blank eyes. Blood everywhere.

Anger welled up inside him and he bit the inside of his cheek to keep his body from trembling, the pain and taste of blood providing a brief antidote.

"That's it for now. I'll let you know when we get anything else," Washburn said.

Ryan stood and gave the detective a half-hearted handshake, letting out a weak, "Thanks."

As he walked through the parking lot, he took all his bottled-up anger and placed it in his right fist. When he got to his car, he unloaded on the rear side panel leaving a large dent. He felt nothing—just shook out his hand, grabbed his keys, jumped in, and peeled out.

The crime scene came to life again in all its technicolor. Then the mugshot filled his mind.

I'm gonna find you Russell Stevens—and I'm gonna kill you.

3

KENNEDY

The repeated "ping" of a utensil on crystal boomed over loudspeakers at an opulent outdoor gathering of 200 guests on the La Jolla Shores bluff. The Pacific sparkled in a perfect sunset as the crowd pushed themselves away from their resplendent tables, wait staff already clearing the cutlery and china, replacing them with coffee and an assortment of delicate French desserts that included tarte tatin, crème brûlée, eclairs, and canelés. Stewards already readied the guests with Dom Pérignon in fluted crystal glasses.

All eyes turned to tall, dark-haired, tuxedoed Logan Young. "I would like to propose a toast," Logan said into the microphone as he raised his glass. He looked down at the crowd from the wedding rehearsal dinner party dais and beamed.

They all stood, their champagne at the ready.

"Three years ago, I met a beautiful girl at a diner in downtown San Diego. I went in there to get a java chiller but stopped in my tracks by the sight of a girl with long brown hair and a dazzling smile. After that, every time I requested the same girl every time."

He paused and winked at Kennedy. She nodded and blushed, her shade matching her stunning couture Vera Wang gown. Completing her look was a fishtail braid adorned with baby's breath, a diamond necklace from Harry Winston, and the heaviest makeup she'd ever worn—compliments of Logan's mother, Linda—she insisted.

Logan reached for Kennedy's hand and she stood. He resumed, "There was just something special about her—aside from her looks. Whatever it was, I seemed to lose all courage when I looked at her. I tried to talk to her for weeks and then finally, one day, I asked her name. I remember the date—how could I forget it? It was Valentines' Day."

Logan paused while the crowd "oohed" and "aahed" about the sweetness of his love story. Someone shouted, "Kiss her already!"

That started up the guests as they chanted, "Kiss her, kiss her."

Logan shrugged his shoulders as if he must appease the crowd, and looked at Kennedy who returned a big smile. He gave her a quick peck on the lips.

A few boos came from the guests, but Logan raised his arms to quiet them. "As many of you know, I was in college at the time, playing basketball and studying. But my grades were affected by this girl. I was scared. Imagine that." He chuckled. "Oh, and her name was Kennedy."

Laughter peppered the crowd, and Kennedy lowered her head in embarrassment.

"A lot has changed in the last three years. I went from being a partying frat boy to a responsible man—and I owe it all to

Kennedy. I'm so excited about our life together." He reached for their glasses, handing one to Kennedy. "To our future. I love you, Kennedy!"

The guests downed their champagne and clapped. Logan and Kennedy stared into each other's eyes, then entwined their arms with their glasses and sipped their champagne.

Logan urged Kennedy toward the microphone and nodded his encouragement.

Reluctantly she spoke, "Tomorrow a new life begins for me—as the wife of Logan Young. I couldn't be happier. Thank you all for coming." She stepped away and looked to him for approval.

She was everything he desired—perfect in so many ways. He took a deep breath and leaned back into the microphone. "Let's get this party started! Everyone to the dance floor where Ludacris will make this place rock!"

Logan and Kennedy led the way into the mansion's ballroom as *Money Maker* blared over the speakers. He held her close as they swayed together on imported Italian marble and under crystal chandeliers adorned with golden silk ribbon streamers. The lights dimmed and two spotlights lit up the betrothed couple.

"You look so beautiful tonight, Kennedy," Logan whispered in her ear. "I really like what my mother did with your hair and makeup."

"Logan, if this is the rehearsal dinner, what's the wedding going to be like tomorrow?"

"Mother took care of everything. It'll be perfect—just like you."

He twirled her, the wine from dinner and the champagne making her dizzy in the most delicious way. Everything was a blur.

In the middle of the song, she spotted a lonely woman in the corner. It had been years since Kennedy last saw her and memories of her youth came rushing back. Miss Betty Old Horn of the Crow Nation still wore her hair in long braids that framed her face and fell to her chest, but they were now gray from the harshness of life on an Indian reservation.

You traveled so far to come here, Kennedy thought.

A ripple of guilt and embarrassment came over Kennedy, but it dissipated as soon as Miss Betty signed [I love you]. Kennedy beamed a grateful smile. When Logan spun her around again, Miss Betty was gone. Kennedy glanced around which threw their rehearsed dance out of balance.

Was it really you?

Logan touched her chin lightly to get her attention. "Hey, Kennedy. Where'd you go?"

She shook her head. "I thought I saw someone I knew, but..." She looked into Logan eyes. "It's nothing. Let's dance."

This was the fairy tale Kennedy knew from every Disney movie, and it was hers. Rich, good-looking Logan Young would make all her dreams come true. First was their honeymoon, a two-week cruise of the Mediterranean, followed by another two weeks of first-class accommodations at five-star hotels and castles throughout Europe. Waiting for them when they returned was the penthouse home of an exclusive new high rise with 360-degree views up and down the coast from La Jolla.

She felt like pinching herself. What impressed her most about Logan was his respect. She saved herself for the man she would marry. That meant there were no long-time boyfriends in her past once they discovered she wouldn't have sex with them. Logan was all right with it, knowing he would be her first—even encouraging that they wait for their wedding night. He was perfect in every way, except for occasionally drinking too much. Kennedy felt that was something they could work on.

At the end of that first song, the 200 guests came onto the dance floor, and one by one, the men tapped each other on the shoulder to cut in for a chance to dance with her. These were people of industry, senators, and congressmen—all with compliments and ogling Kennedy, something she wasn't accustomed to, but her low cut Vera Wang commanded attention. She was relieved, when after a dozen or so men danced with her, Logan rescued her from the dance floor, leading her to a table set aside just for them.

"Thank you," a breathless Kennedy said. She noticed two empty wine glasses being carted away by the wait staff, and two fresh glasses appearing. "You shouldn't—"

Logan cut her off, handing her a glass and lifting his to his lips. "Don't go worrying about how much I drink. Not tonight, honey."

"But you know how you can—"

"I'll be fine. Now drink up." He tapped her glass playfully. "This is three hundred dollars a bottle. We're celebrating."

She took a long sip and her eyes widened in surprise. "Whoa, this is good."

"You have another hundred men to dance with, so you need your strength." He laughed.

Kennedy leaned into Logan so no one could hear. "I don't like the way they're all looking at me—in this dress. And I'm not wearing a bra."

"That's the way the dress is designed. Besides it looks beautiful on you, and you've got a gorgeous body." He drained his glass and pulled her onto the dance floor. "Ready to party?"

She didn't have time to blush as he spun her around.

After an hour, when the band took a break, she found Logan sitting with a group of his high finance co-workers at a table across the room and came up behind him.

He leaned back in his chair, an empty wine glass in his hand. "I told her when we first started dating, once I graduated and landed a job, I would marry the shit out of her!"

The men burst into laughter.

"Well, here I am! Tomorrow is the day!"

Kennedy flushed and cleared her throat. Logan turned, wrapped an arm around her waist and forced her on his lap, his face level with her chest.

"Logan," she said, trying to be polite around his friends, but feeling awkward. She pushed his shoulders lightly trying to appear playful.

A voice from another table let out, "Why don't you two make some babies!"

You're all drunk.

He pushed her off his lap with, "I wanna make an announcement. Come on."

He pulled her over to the stage and waved at the band to stop. "Take a break, okay?"

Logan approached the microphone. "I would like to thank everyone for coming out, and especially Linda Logan, my mother, for putting this wonderful night together for us. You don't know how much Kennedy and I appreciate everything you've done for us." Logan took another sip of wine. "And if anyone needs a lawyer, Linda Logan is the best in California— hell, the best in the country!"

Logan squinted his blue eyes, trying to see his mother through the spotlights. He waved to Linda to come up and the crowd's applause moved her forward.

Kennedy felt the room shrink when Linda walked toward the stage, the crowd parting. It was as if she was a giant towering over her guests. Her frame was muscular and toned due to her daily workouts with her personal trainer with everything from Pilates to Yoga. She wore a couture gown, her sun-streaked hair in perfect ringlets that bounced off her shoulders—to rival Kennedy in every way. Everyone stopped what they were doing, even the waiters.

Linda began, "I am so honored you could attend my only son, Logan's wedding. A few of you traveled across several oceans and continents to make this special day even more special for me."

As she went on naming the notables and celebrities in the ballroom, Kennedy noticed Logan sway. She wrapped an arm around him to steady him. She nudged when he took his seat and she gave him a disapproving face he knew all too well.

He leaned in and whispered, "It's fine babe, just a little wine. It's a night of celebration." He raised his glass and took another long gulp.

"I know, and that's fine, but I want our wedding to be perfect. I just want you at your best tomorrow." She smiled politely knowing people watched them.

"You are so considerate babe, but I'm fine." He took another sip and kissed her sloppily dragging his lips across her cheek.

She saw this a few times before, remnants of his college days. She gave herself a pep talk.

Come on, Kennedy. Just make it through tonight and tomorrow.

She was going to marry the only man she had ever known to love her, even if the party and people weren't her taste. She loved this moment. She loved the fact that Logan loved her irrespective of her class and status. He was truly a gentleman in her eyes. He chose her without even thinking about her background and the poverty she came from. She loved the perfect, blissful, euphoria she felt with Logan. And she loved the way Logan sheltered her and made her feel secure and safe.

In Logan's world, everything was different. Kennedy adapted to this change, considering it a small price for finding the true love of her life.

The night came to an end and they took a limo to the U.S. Grant Hotel, where the penthouse suite waited for them. Their last night together before matrimony. They made their way to the elevator, Logan stumbling with Kennedy not much help, and punched the up button. From the bar off the lobby, a DJ played an old R&B song about a pony. Logan burst into song, trying to hit the high notes, singing at the top of his lungs. For some reason, Kennedy found herself laughing hysterically. The elevator doors opened and they stumbled in.

It was difficult getting the key to work for the penthouse, but they prevailed, giggling as they entered.

As she headed towards the bathroom, he grabbed her by the wrist. "No."

"What? I want to get this makeup off my face," she slurred.

He pulled her close and tightened his grip. She was confused and tried to playfully slap him on the chest. His hold became stronger and she winced because of the pain. "You're hurting me."

"Calm down, I just want to help you get out of your dress."

Sobering up, she said, "Thank you, but it's okay. I'll take it off in the bathroom when I put on my pajamas."

Logan's tone shifted. "No. I'll do it." He grabbed her zipper, and yanked it down.

Kennedy softened her voice to counter his aggression. "Come on, honey. You know our arrangement." She tried to pull her dress back up.

"I don't care. I want to be inside you."

"We've talked about this. Just one more day," she pleaded.

"Honey … we're basically married. What's a couple hours?" He pawed at her.

"No! Not until we're married." She stepped back.

Logan's eyes went wild. He yanked her dress off, and she fell back on the bed, wearing only her panties.

She let out a little yelp and grabbed a pillow to cover herself. "What're you doing? You're drunk."

He looked at her with lustful eyes and a contorted grin, then took off his pants and kicked off his shoes. No words would come from this crazed man.

He grabbed her legs and pulled her across the comforter to him.

"Stop, Logan! This isn't like you!"

He ripped off her panties, then he climbed on her, forcing her legs apart with his knees.

One last plea of "No," escaped her lips.

He entered her, slamming his body into hers. The image of a white devil and a red river flashed across her mind—an old native tale from her past. It disappeared when he put a hand over her mouth as she screamed. He thrust his hips harder as she tried to squirm away. After agonizing minutes of relentless assault, he made one final lunge accompanied by a loud grunt, and rolled off of her, immediately falling asleep.

Kennedy curled up in a ball and gasped, trying to calm her throbbing body, tears flooding her eyes. Her first impulse was to run away—far away—to a place he'd never find. She stayed that way for an hour, the hall light casting shadows over the shame and horror of his act.

She rolled over, clutching her stomach, and looked at Logan's peaceful face. "You love me, don't you," she whispered. It was both a question and a hope.

Kennedy quietly showered, a trickle of blood running down her legs, a stark reminder of what just happened. As she toweled off, she found herself staring into the mirror. The heavy makeup

Logan's mother applied made her look like a whore. She scrubbed it off, then put on her pajamas, and sat on the sofa across from the bed where Logan slept peacefully. Her tears began again.

It was supposed to be special.

She stared at the ceiling in silence until her eyes hurt with a thousand unanswered questions. If she canceled the wedding, what would happen to her? She quit her job, moved out of her apartment, and Logan bought her a Porsche. She lost herself somewhere along the way. He owned her.

Maybe he won't always be like this.

From deep inside her, just before dawn, a resolve took hold.

I will marry you, Logan Young.

4

RYAN

Ryan swung by the 'death house' to gauge if he was ready to retrieve the few items he wanted to keep. He held the key in his hand, rubbing the dull brass with his thumb, imaging the tumblers of the lock engaging, the click of the front door, and swinging it open—*I can't.*

He unpacked the mail box, stuffed with two weeks' worth of mail. He contacted the post office to have all the mail forwarded to Aunt Morgan's. Utilities, land rental, house payments, HOA fees, insurance, property taxes—he never knew there was so much to owning a home. He let the unopened envelopes, with their "You've Already Won" and "overdue" notices stamped in bright red, pile up in a shoe box in the corner of his bedroom—like the way he piled up his anger—unanswered.

***

Ever since Aunt Morgan's husband died in Vietnam 45 years before, she worked as a secretary at a construction company. She got Ryan summer jobs there doing demolition and general cleanup of properties before they were renovated. A month after the funeral, he started up with them again part time.

The small crew consisted mostly of older Mexicans where Ryan's high school Spanish came in handy.

His first job was renovating a 50-room motel conversion. They were going to make 25 condos out of it. Joe Watson, the foreman, handed Ryan a pry bar, sledgehammer, and some goggles, and told him to rip out the dry wall down to the studs for ten rooms.

He waved his large hairy arms. "Plumbing fixtures, lights, windows, and insulation are getting replaced, so no need to be careful. Power's shut off and so's the water, so let her rip," Joe said grinning. "I'll call you for lunch."

"Okay," Ryan answered. He glanced around at the bare walls and floor, the carpet already gone. He adjusted his goggles, looked up at the popcorn ceiling, put in his earbuds, and hefted the sledgehammer. Fifty Cent's *Hate It Love It* flooded his ears as he took his first swing.

***

Even though it was February in Michigan and all the windows and door were open, Ryan's jacket was off and his shirt drenched with sweat from pounding and ripping out walls for hours. A tap on his shoulder startled him. He turned to find Joe speaking but couldn't hear him until he pulled off his head phones.

"What?" Ryan asked.

"Lunch time. You bring anything?"

Ryan took off his goggles and gloves, shaking his head.

"Didn't think so." Joe tossed him a brown lunch bag and smiled. "Your aunt packed something for you. Come on."

Ryan followed Joe to a downstairs room where the rest of the small crew, a white guy and four Mexicans, sat on five-gallon buckets with lunch pails by their boots already chowing down. A small boom box in the corner blared mariachi music. Ryan grabbed a bottled water, found a bucket, and opened his lunch bag to find two ham sandwiches and an apple.

He hadn't thought about his folks once during the morning—and that was good.

This is what I needed. Pound walls. Forget.

Halfway through his second sandwich, a playful shove to Ryan's shoulder brought him out of his thoughts. He looked over at the white man, mid-40s, dirty moustache.

Dark brown hair spilled from under his hardhat. "You the new guy?" the white guy asked wiping his hands on his stained blue coveralls.

"I guess I am. Why?"

"Nothing. Billy." He stuck out a dirty hand to Ryan.

"Ryan," as he responded with a courtesy shake.

"So, what's a good lookin' young buck doin' in a shit hole like this?"

Ryan looked over at Joe and got a shrug that said *That's Billy.*

Billy continued. "Pay's shit, ya know. My old lady's always bitching about that. But fuck that fat bitch, most of it goes towards strippers and beer. I stimulate the economy, if you know what I mean."

Ryan winced out a small courtesy grin not wanting to encourage him.

"If I was a young buck like you, I'd be dropping my kiddos off at one of those sperm clinics, ya know what I'm saying," he chuckled and slapped Ryan's back. "Shit, I probably got a hundred kids runnin' around with moms that are 100 pounds skinnier than my old lady. By the way, don't get married, it's a trick."

Billy stood and stretched.

"You want all of those kids living around you in your own hometown?" Ryan asked.

"Fuck no, that'd creep me out. It doesn't work that way. They send those skeet cups all over the country. Totally anonymous."

"Okay," Joe barked. "Break's over. Let's get back to it."

***

At the end of the day, Billy approached Ryan in the parking lot. "The good thing about construction is that you start early and end early—but it's the starting early that sucks." He smile and paused. "Hey, you comin' for a beer and to chase some skirt over at O'Malley's?"

"No. Got some things to do," said Ryan as he waved him off and jumped in his car. He'd left his phone in his car and checked for messages—he had two voicemails.

Now what?

The first was from the funeral home. "Mr. Turner. We haven't received your payment this month. That's two months now. We have you on a payment plan that doesn't include interest. Please call us."

Shit. Where am I gonna get seven thousand dollars?

The second voicemail was from Detective Washburn. A simple, "Call me back," was all he said, but it was the way he said it.

Ryan's hands shook as he dialed the direct number.

"Washburn. How can I help you?"

"It's Ryan, Ryan Turner."

"We caught him—Russell Stevens."

The crime scene came back to life with all its dark red and chaos. The black and white mug shot, then the unspeakable picture of his mother and father on their kitchen floor. While the detective went on about Russell's arrest in Chicago and extraditing him, Ryan started to cry.

The detective finished with, "Well, that's it. I just wanted to let you know. He confessed. It's over."

"Thanks," Ryan whispered, hung up, and slumped onto the steering wheel.

Half an hour later when he went to start his car—nothing— not even a *click* to make him feel like there was some life left in his old heap.

Fuck.

The tow to a local repair shop cost him a hundred fifty bucks which he barely managed to put on his only credit card. The estimate to repair the faded green Ford Escort added another $1,200 to the tally of his life. A dull resignation came over Ryan as he stood at the grease-stained counter of repair shop.

"You want it?" Ryan asked.

"Want what?" the repair man asked.

"My car. I can't afford the repairs."

I can't afford anything.

"I can set you up on a payment plan and—"

"It's yours." He separated the key from the ring that held two door keys—his parents' and Aunt Morgan's. He slapped it on the counter.

The repair shop owner looked over at the Escort then back to Ryan. "Okay, but you'll need to sign some papers."

Ryan nodded. "Just let me get some stuff out of the car."

Between the glove box, under the seats, and trunk, he gathered gloves, a hard hat, a pair of vice grips, an old sleeping bag, a black beanie, two pairs of scratched sunglasses, a collection of dead lotto tickets, and his student ID. He studied the smiling face on the photo.

You were so different then.

He took the gloves, hard hat, and beanie—slamming the car door with a finality, his past shuttered behind faded green metal and glass.

Ryan signed the title transfer and walked out to the sidewalk. He looked down at his phone—4:33. The dark and cold were taking over the day. Ryan put on the beanie and hard hat and gloves, flipped up his collar and started the long walk home. The outside lights went on in a strip mall across the street and Ryan stopped when he saw the "Military Recruiting" sign. He looked up and down the street, back at the repair shop, and hurried across the street.

***

Four recruiting desks were manned by the four branches of the military with posters of tall, young, chiseled Marines, Navy, Air Force, or Army recruits looking as if they were embarking on the adventure of a lifetime. Unlike his uncle who died in

Vietnam, or his father who was wounded there, both fighting in the Army, he picked the Marines.

After an hour of going over the different options available for a 20-year-old high school graduate, Ryan nodded his head. "Sounds good."

You'll be my family now.

"You'll receive your ten thousand dollar enlistment bonus after you complete basic training. If that works for you, sign here and we'll schedule your physical," the starched Marine sergeant said pointing to the enlistment form. The name stitched above his right pocket read "Garrison."

Without hesitation, Ryan scribbled his name and bobbed his head in approval.

"Welcome to the U.S. Marines, soldier," Sergeant Garrison said.

The sergeant and Ryan stood and shook hands. Ryan almost saluted but didn't know how. When he walked outside, he stood a little taller—something about taking control of a life that was aimless and out of control. His thoughts went to his father's limp, especially when colder weather set in like it was today.

Not what you wanted for me, but I'm gonna be a Marine, Dad.

He called Aunt Morgan. "Hey, I'm going to be a little late—and I've got some really good news."

She heard the excitement in his voice. "I put a meatloaf in the oven. It should be ready in an hour or so. You can tell me all about it then."

***

The news about the arrest of Russell Stevens struck her hard—a name now linked to the murder of her brother and his wife. Ryan reached for some Kleenex from the counter as her tears started.

After several moments, he shoveled some food in his mouth. "This meatloaf is great, Aunt Morgan. I mean, it's really good."

She sniffled and wiped her nose. "It's nice to cook for someone other than just myself. I forgot how much I missed the company. So, tell me, how was your first day on the job? Did Joe take care of you alright?"

"Yeah, and thanks for the lunch."

She blushed a little, reached over and patted Ryan's arm. "It's nothing."

"Well, I won't be working there much longer—I joined the Marines today."

"What?" She straightened, sitting up.

"I'll be going to basic thirty days after my physical."

"Why, with what happened to my husband and Alvin..." her voice trailed off.

"When I get out, I'll have the GI Bill so I can go back to college." He tried his best to sound upbeat.

"I was just getting used to having a man around the house." She set down her fork and sat back in her chair.

"I'll write. And before I go, I'll show you how to do Skype and email so we can stay in touch. You're the only family I got." He took a hard swallow as the words hit him.

"Oh, I don't know much about computers and all."

"I'll teach you. It's gonna be fun."

***

With his car gone, he drove Aunt Morgan to work in her car and headed to over to the renovation project. He thanked Joe for the job and told him about his plans.

"I hope things work out." Joe raised his voice so the other men could hear. "You're the best worker I've had in a *long* time."

The crew of Mexicans and Billy picked up their pace, some shooting Ryan brief head shakes.

***

When Ryan returned home, he brought the mail from his bedroom to the kitchen, emptying the box onto the kitchen table. Using a steak knife, he opened all the prize letters and bills and sorted them out. He dug into Aunt Morgan's desk to find a pad and pen and a calculator. It took him three hours, but he had it all down in black and white.

Between the money owed the mortuary and all the bills associated with his parents' home, it totaled almost $11,000.

First thing, I gotta turn off the utilities and sell the place— if anyone'll take it.

He found himself doodling and tapping his pen trying to figure out his next move when his phone rang. He looked at the caller ID—Pearson Mortuary.

Shit.

He answered, "Ryan Turner."

"Mr. Turner, we've sent you notices and left you messages without any response. I know this must be a difficult time for you, but we need you to make a payment."

"I'll have the entire amount in three months." There was no response. "Uh, do you take credit cards?"

"Yes, and I can take down your number over the phone."
Ryan didn't respond. "I'm ready when you are?"

Ryan pulled the credit card out his wallet and stared at it,
knowing the towing fee had maxed it out. "I'll have to call you
back."

"Mr. Turner, if we don't hear back from you this week,
we're turning this over to a collection agency."

Why don't you get your blood money from Russell Stevens?

"I understand." Ryan hung up and looked at the piles of
bills.

One at time. Just do one at a time.

By late that afternoon, he turned off the utilities and talked
to the bank about the loan on his parents' home, realizing it was
easier to walk from the property, with its second mortgage, than
try to make the payments—besides, he could never live there
again.

Ryan called the Marine recruiter. "Sergeant Garrison, this
is Ryan Turner."

"You haven't changed your mind, have you, Ryan?"

"No, no. I wanted to schedule my physical as soon as
possible."

"How does tomorrow morning at nine at MRD sound?"

"Great. Just send me directions."

After he hung up, he placed another call.

"Fertility Center of California, Sperm Bank. How may I
help you?" a professional female voice answered.

"Uh, I heard you pay for samples—from healthy young
men…" he didn't know quite how to say it.

"Our offices are located on 6699 Alvarado. You can come in any time for an evaluation."

"Expect to see me tomorrow afternoon."

***

Following his *deposit* into a sterile plastic cup, Ryan shared the waiting room with a number of women who carried a sense of desperation, their eyes nervously scanning magazines. Ryan checked his phone for messages and email, already one from the Marines—he passed the physical.

In the middle of a deep sigh of relief, his name was called and he followed a nurse into a doctor's office and told to wait. Pictures of smiling couples holding Gerber babies were tastefully scattered across the walls.

The doctor, a smiling 50-ish woman with short brown hair entered and took a seat behind her neat desk. She held a report.

"Mr. Turner, I'm glad to say you're an excellent donor."

Ryan nodded sheepishly, recalling the magazines he looked through before settling on a picture of a younger version of the doctor bent over a desk looking back at him and smiling.

"You have one of the highest sperm counts we've seen. Coupled with your physique, IQ, and family history, well, we'd like you to consider signing up for our monthly donation. We can pay you $1,500 to make two deposits a week—eight in all for the month."

"Let's do a month. I'm planning on taking a trip after that."

"Okay then, let's sign you up."

***

Driving over to pick up Aunt Morgan, he grinned thinking how he could possibly explain to her what he'd done.

They paid me to look at pictures of naked ladies and jerk off. Maybe I can sell my blood next. At least all my bills will get paid.

5

RYAN

Ryan thought hell week with the Kalamazoo High Hornet's football team was tough—two-a-days in muggy heat, relentless drills, always ending with a mile run in full gear. Like most teenagers, he didn't truly appreciate his mother's cooking at the time, the simple comfort of a warm shower, a soft bed with clean sheets, and getting eight hours of sleep.

Thirteen weeks at MCRD San Diego for Marine Corps basic training was nothing like football. *Relentless* was the word that came to Ryan's when reveille blared at four a.m. and drill sergeants screamed, "Eyes forward." "Drop and give me twenty, Turner."

Ryan loved the physical challenge, but what drove him every step of the way was the image of Russell Stevens—and what he did to his parents. Like a tall Oak, Ryan grew deep roots of hatred for the man who took everything he loved. If he couldn't kill Russell Stevens, then he'd kill the Taliban or anyone else the Marine Corps put in front of him.

Thirteen weeks filled with thousands of "Yes, Sir!", push ups, sit ups, pull ups, a bed made so tight you could bounce a quarter off it, hand-to-hand combat, shooting, and polishing brass and boots to a see-your-reflection shine. When it was over, Ryan bested everyone in his unit's obstacle course, and was the company's expert marksman, scoring 249 of 250. Stationary targets were easy to hit—nothing like shooting deer and elk on bone-chilling mornings with his father in the Upper Peninsula of Michigan.

Thanks, Dad.

He was told to report to Colonel Masterson, the second in command at the Marine Corps boot camp. After he was led into the room by the colonel's sergeant, Ryan lifted his hand in a crisp salute and waited. The colonel was lean, about six feet tall, with a scar that ran from the tip of his chin to the middle of his cheekbone. Hard eyes. A warrior. He returned the salute.

Now, why am I here?

"At ease, Turner. Take a seat."

A file was open on the colonel's desk and Ryan could tell it was his.

"Seems like you made a good impression on your instructors, Turner. You have…" he looked down, did a double-take, then looked up, "some remarkable results. In fact, I don't believe I've ever seen such marks."

"Thank you, Sir." Ryan remained seated at attention.

"You were one point away from a perfect score on the range."

"Yes, Sir. I believe that is correct."

"It says here you started college but didn't complete it."

"Yes, Sir."

"I only ask in case you have difficulty with classroom work."

"No, Sir. I don't have any difficulty." Ryan paused, thinking back to how alive he felt that one week at Eastern Michigan, his future full of possibilities. He shoved the memory back down to his roots. "I had to drop out due to—family circumstances."

"Yes, that can happen. Well, after your ten-day leave, you'll be reporting to SOI for nine weeks of training at Camp Pendleton. If you continue doing well, don't be surprised if you're approached to *volunteer* for some special assignments." The colonel grinned but seeing Ryan's stiff demeanor added, "This is a good thing, Turner. Any questions."

"Yes, Sir." Ryan cleared his throat. "If I may, Sir, Gunny said it might be possible—I'd like to forgo my leave and enter SOI now."

The colonel let out a broad smile. "That'd be just fine, Turner."

"One more thing, if I may, Sir?"

The colonel nodded for Ryan to continue.

"Now that I've completed basic, when will my sign-up bonus be available? I want it sent to my aunt."

"Not your folks?"

His parents' bloody bodies on their kitchen floor rushed into his mind. He shook his head to clear it away. "No, my aunt."

"Talk to Sergeant Dawson. He'll take care of everything." The colonel stood and held out his hand. "Welcome aboard, Marine."

Ryan stood and shook it. "Thank you, Sir." He saluted and it was returned.

The colonel yelled, "Dawson." The door opened and his sergeant appeared to escort Ryan out.

***

The Marine Corps' SOI—the School of Infantry was located in Oceanside, California. It would be nine weeks of training before Ryan received his first assignment and he was anxious to get going. His two weeks in the classroom were like being back in college—except for the coeds. They covered customs and courtesies, first aid, marine corps history, terrorism awareness, leadership, official policies and organizational values, and operational risk management. It was a lot to digest and Ryan's brain got a complete workout.

Seven weeks of field work included training in all sorts of arms—rifles, machine guns, mortars, and anti-tank missiles—all the while juggling intense physical training. Wedged into this, Ryan got to fire an M40, the rifle used by Scout Snipers. He liked the weight and feel of the rifle, the recoil, the hints of hot oil and gunpowder swirling in air around him—but mostly he liked Russell Stevens' head in the center of each target. He finished first in his unit.

The SOI recruits ended their nine-week course with a grueling 20-kilometer hike. His unit's commander asked to see Ryan. He wasn't as nervous as when Colonel Masterson called him into his office.

"How's Bud doing, Turner?" Colonel Diller asked, an unlit cigar hanging out the side of his mouth, graying hair in a high-and-tight buzz cut, and the most ribbons Ryan's ever saw on a uniform. Ryan's file, thicker now, rested on Colonel Diller's desk.

Ryan answered "Sir?" and wrinkled his brow.

"Oh, Colonel Bud Masterson. How's he doing?"

"Fine, I suppose, Sir."

"Well, Bud has some very good things to say about you. You impressed him, Turner. Me as well. Your orders have come down and I think you'll like them." He teased Ryan's curiosity by smiling and drumming his fingers on Ryan's file. "Want to know?"

"If you'd like to tell me, yes, Sir, that would be nice."

"You'll be headed to MCB Hawaii—and not for surfing lessons."

He let out a little laugh and Ryan grinned in response.

"Kaneohe Bay's Regimental School runs a 10-week Scout Sniper school. This is an elite group, Turner, and an honor. I can't count the number of times my unit's sniper saved my sorry ass in combat and the men in my command. Do us proud, son."

"I'll do my best, Sir."

6

KENNEDY

K ennedy glided past the open French doors onto the expansive penthouse patio overlooking La Jolla Cove, holding a tray filled with a resplendent Sunday morning breakfast. A homemade pimento and shitake mushroom quiche, fresh fruit, croissants, and a pot of Kopi Luwak Gold coffee—everything the way Logan liked it. The hazy sun found him at their bistro table in a red silk robe and sunglasses, his Mont Blanc pen busy filling in squares on the New York Times' crossword.

"Ready, honey?" Kennedy asked.

Logan didn't answer, too absorbed in his challenge. He prided himself in solving it in under fifteen minutes. She paused to take him in—tall, handsome—but so different from the man she married eight months ago. This one erupted in anger at the slightest provocation, especially when he had a bad day trading stocks, or if he drank too much—or that Kennedy wasn't pregnant yet.

She set the tray on the edge of the table. "Logan, honey? It'll get cold."

He looked up at her with a frown, then at his Rolex, and closed the paper with a snort. "Just coffee."

Kennedy poured him a steaming cup, set her plate on the table, and sat down. She started in on her slice of quiche, avoiding the pimentos. It was easier to avoid the pimentos than Logan's disappointment if they were missing.

A small gathering of green parrots in a nearby palm sang out. Kennedy smiled, taking them in. "It's so nice out here, with the birds and—"

"What's so nice about them? All they do is shit on our Brown Jordan furniture." He grabbed the croissant off Kennedy's plate and heaved it at the tree, the birds scattering.

You're in one of your moods. What is it now?

She reached over and placed a calm hand on his shoulder but he shrugged it off.

Logan turned on her. "You know I want a child."

"I'm trying. I really am." Kennedy lowered her fork and sat rigid, trying to remain neutral, not giving Logan more to get upset about.

"I told you before we got married, I wanted children. I wouldn't have married you if you couldn't bear a child."

Kennedy's mind filled with memories of their sex life, her virginity lost to his drunken rape the night before they married, to every time after with his more and more degrading sex acts. He insisted she watch porno films with him and forced her to try what they saw. She felt a lump in her throat and tears building up. She looked away. "I keep taking the tests…" her voice trailed off.

"That's not good enough! I've given you everything—look around you. I work hard so you can be a stay at home mother. I want a child, damn it!" He slammed his hand on the table, his coffee cup spilling. He pushed himself away from the table and stormed into the house.

Kennedy lost her appetite and sat alone for several minutes. She sighed, wiped the table and cleared up the dishes, quietly bringing them to the kitchen.

Logan was in the living room loading a backpack with a gallon of water and energy bars, then slipped on his new hiking shoes. He looked at her with disdain. "Do we really have to go hiking, Kennedy? I mean, really?"

"You promised. And besides, we barely do anything together. Please."

"Okay, whatever," he rolled his eyes. "Where is this Three Sister's thing anyway—and when you gonna be ready?" He switched on the TV.

"It's so beautiful there. I'll be ready in ten minutes and it's out in the east country, only half an hour away."

"Well then, let's get going," he snorted.

"It'll be fun to see how your Porsche Cayenne handles bumpy dirt roads."

"Yeah. I'll have to get it detailed after and probably have to take it in to check for realignment."

Kennedy ignored him and went to the bedroom to change. She took her long black hair, made into two braids, then tied them together and covered them with a floppy hat. She was back in 10 minutes, Logan already absorbed in a movie. She tried to sound chipper. "Those boots look really nice on you, honey."

He gave her *the look*, switched off the TV, and pointed to the backpack. "That's yours."

***

They drove in silence but Kennedy didn't mind, the excitement of being outdoors taking her back to her childhood when she lived on the Crow Indian Reservation in Montana. The land was sacred to her, the lore passed down to her as a child by tribal elders, held deep in her heart.

She was jolted out of her daydream by Logan's voice yelling, "What the fuck?"

She looked up to find the freeway clogged and a faded blue Chevy Impala in front of them driving five miles an hour under the speed limit. They were boxed in.

"How the fuck did you get a driver's license?"

Kennedy inched away from Logan and tensed. He swerved into another lane cutting off another driver who honked. Logan flipped him off in his rearview mirror. The driver in front of them was an older lady. He revved his engine, coming within inches of her bumper and braking.

Kennedy gripped her seat belt, her heart thumping in her chest.

What are you going to do now?

"What the fuck?!" Logan continued. He looked to his right and left to see if he could get around her—not looking up in time to avoid plowing into her, the Porsche rocking to a hard stop.

"Goddammit. Stupid fucking bitch," the words exploded and kept coming. He rolled down his window waved to have her pull over to the side of the road.

He took a few deep breaths, ran his hands through his hair, let out a few more cuss words directed at the old lady, and stepped out of his car. He turned back to Kennedy. "Watch me charm the old bag."

He inspected his Porsche, not a scratch. The old lady exited her car and walked to the back. She seemed fine but her bumper dangled by a wire. Kennedy rolled down her window to listen.

Putting on his best Logan smile, he asked the old lady, "I'm so sorry. Are you okay?"

She nodded but then she looked at her bumper. "Oh, my."

Kennedy strained to hear the rest of their conversation but couldn't make out anything. Logan placed a comforting hand on the old lady's shoulder. After some gentle talking, he bent down and pulled the bumper off the old lady's car, put it in her trunk, opened his wallet and handed her a wad of cash. She nodded and smiled, went back to her car, started it up and pulled away. Logan waved.

Logan hopped back in his SUV and snarled, "This little outing of yours just cost us an extra thousand dollars. I can hardly wait to see what happens next."

Ten minutes later they exited and stopped by a bait and tackle shop to get an adventure pass. Kennedy paid for it.

Five minutes later, they were on a bumpy dirt road, winding through foothills.

"This SUV really handles this nice," Kennedy said, trying again to sound chipper.

His only comment was a grunt.

They arrived at the trail head on Boulder Creek Road in a dirty vehicle, Logan taking a swipe of the hood and shaking his head. They unloaded their gear and placed the adventure pass on the dash. Logan handed the heavy backpack to Kennedy. She looked at him, a small plea in her eyes.

"You're the one who wanted this hike, and since you're the half breed, you get to carry the pack," Logan smirked.

She looked at him with his board shorts, tank top, Raybans, and Nike boots. *You don't know how to do this.* She wore khaki pants with a sports bra, floppy hat, windbreaker, and Northface boots.

"Okay." Kennedy hoisted the pack. "So you know, getting to Three Sisters Falls is a bit of a hike, one of the hardest in the area."

He smirked. "If you can do it, I can handle it."

"Well, let's get going then." She headed off at a quick pace and smiled to herself as Logan struggled to keep up.

At the trail junction, they headed downhill skipping past the Eagles Peak turnout. They were picking their way through a series of small boulders, when Logan let loose with a shriek. Kennedy turned to see him stumble backwards and she grinned.

"What happened?" she called out.

He pointed down at the trail with a shaky finger. "It's—it's a tarantula."

She walked back, bent down and let the tarantula crawl onto her hand.

"How can you do that? Isn't it poisonous?" he nearly screamed.

"No, silly. Only the ones from South America have venom." She held out her hand. "Want to pet it?"

"Ugh," he answered, scurried around her, and headed down the trail.

She smiled, the first time today. She put the hairy spider on a nearby boulder. "Thanks," she whispered to it and took off after Logan.

The sky was a sparkling blue, the freshest air she breathed in the last eight months. This was her in the elements, perfect. A half hour later, they came upon their first obstacle—a steep slope requiring them to scale down it using a dangling guide rope.

"It doesn't look safe," Logan moaned.

Kennedy walked past him, took hold of the rope and walked down the steep path. Logan reluctantly followed, complaining that he should have brought gloves.

A short while later, they came upon another rope climb but it wasn't as steep or long. A half mile further down the trail, they ran into the large boulders that made up most of the river bed of the falls. Here the desert came to life and everything flourished. In the distance they heard a low rumble.

"What's that?" Logan asked.

"The falls. We're almost there."

Rounding a bend, Three Sisters Falls roared to life, with a large natural pool below filled with algae and plants. They walked past the first two falls and found their way to the edge of a stream feeding the third pool.

Kennedy dropped her backpack, stripped down to her sports bra and panties, took off her hat and boots, and jumped in with a loud, "Woo-hoo!"

Logan took a seat on a large boulder and scanned the surroundings for leering eyes. After a few minutes, he grabbed a towel from the backpack and summoned Kennedy over, his jealousy apparent. "You don't want people looking at you."

"I don't mind," Kennedy said. "You should come in, it's refreshing."

Logan waved the towel like he was a matador, his face scrunched in a scowl.

Kennedy dried herself and wrapped the towel around her. "Come on, let's explore the caves."

"We should have something to eat and head back," he commanded.

"We just got here." She dropped the towel and reached for her pants. "We came all this way."

"Yes, and it'll take us just long to get back. I don't want to stay out here all day. Let's go."

You don't know how to have fun.

She knew his mind was made up. They sat on a large boulder overlooking the pond, downed some water, and ate energy bars—all in silence.

She attempted to start up a conversation. "You know, this is part of Cleveland National Forest preserved by Theodore Roosevelt in 1908."

"Who cares." Logan stood. "Come on."

Heading out of the falls, he picked up a long stick.

No doubt to smack any tarantulas who scare you.

When they got to the ropes, he began to whine again, having to pull himself up the long slope. She watched him from below.

I hope you fall and break a leg.

She was surprised by the thought, shook her head, grabbed the rope, and followed Logan up the rise.

They returned to their car five hours after they left it. Logan opened the passenger door and plopped in, reclining the seat—while Kennedy put everything away.

"That was okay," he said in a calm voice.

She started up their Porsche and patted him on the leg. "You did good today, honey. Thanks."

She was answered by Logan's deep breath as he fell asleep.

***

She pulled the Porsche into the garage of their luxury townhouse. Logan stirred awake when she turned off the engine. He leaned over and gave Kennedy a peck on the cheek. Looking in her eyes, he smiled. "It was nice getting out and doing something with you today. Thanks for insisting I go with you."

She beamed. "I thought you might like it."

He lugged the backpack from the car to their penthouse, even opening the door for her.

"Thank you."

You're being so nice.

After he closed the door, he wrapped an arm around her and pulled her into him. "I'm going to get cleaned up. Maybe we can watch some porn and do some baby making."

That grin. Hope drained from her face, knowing what came next.

Not tonight, please.

"I'm a little tired, honey. Can we make love tomorrow?"

"You're ovulating now. We're gonna fuck."

She pushed him away and sized him up again—six-foot, two inches, college football player. She was five-foot three, a hundred five pounds.

She tried to placate him. "How about some wine, maybe watch a movie, and see what happens?"

His eyes went wild. The same look he had the night before their wedding.

"Okay, I'll get cleaned up." She stepped into the bedroom before he had a chance to react and locked the door.

Logan must have heard the click. He tried the doorknob then pounded on the door. "You're gonna have my baby!" he yelled. The door frame bent as he bashed into the door. "Open up!"

"Go away!" Kennedy pleaded.

She bit her lip and frantically looked around for somewhere to hide—she chose the floor on the other side of their bed—her head pressed against the carpet.

"If I have to break down the door, you're gonna pay!"

Kennedy trembled as she waited.

Boom! The door shook as Logan threw his body into it. It became eerily quiet until a final CRACK broke the frame and the door flew open.

"Where are you?" he screamed.

"Stop, Logan! Please."

He looked around and grabbed her perfumes off the dresser, throwing them against the wall above the headboard, filling the room with shards of glass and exotic scents. He bent down, saw her on the floor on the other side of the bed, and flipped the mattress onto her.

She crawled out from under it and scrambled to her feet.

"There you are!" he laughed wickedly.

She ran toward the bathroom, but he grabbed her by her braided hair and dragged her over to the mattress. She screeched when he flipped her onto her stomach. He pulled her hiking pants down to her ankles and ripped off her panties. Kennedy squirmed saying over and over, "No, Logan, not like this. No. No."

He leaned forward and pressed his hand into the back of her head making her look away as he unzipped his pants. He slammed into her, the pain never ceasing as he grunted like a dog. "Take it bitch. Take it all," he yelled.

She struggled against him as he moved her into different positions that excited him, but always held a tight a grip on her neck. Letting out a loud groan and final thrusts, he dumped his seed inside her. Panting, he fell out of her and pulled up his pants. She lay on the bed, low sobs racking her body.

He stopped at the bedroom door. "Have the repairman fix this tomorrow. And make sure he removes the lock."

Kennedy remained motionless for several minutes. She heard Logan turn on the TV, a football game, and rummage around the kitchen for something to eat.

She staggered to the bathroom and took a hot shower, hoping the water would purge the memories. As she toweled off, she stopped—inspecting herself in the full-length mirror. Bruises were forming on her neck and an aching soreness ran through her body. She shuddered.

Kennedy put on her pajamas and walked over to the bed. She looked at the mattress on the floor, the covers askew. She gathered the sheets and blankets into a cocoon and curled up. One question filled her head as she thought of her upbringing as a Crow by Miss Betty Old Horn, her grandmother.

What would you guide me to do?
Kennedy fell into a dark, fitful sleep.

7

RYAN

Through military bus windows pitted by too many sand storms, Ryan watched ragged children laugh and kick a soccer ball around on the side of the road to the base. The bus wound its way past barriers to the entrance of Forward Operating Base Delaram, *Home of the Darkside* the sign read. This is where his second tour in Afghanistan would start. Snow flurries caused the MPs to blink as they walked out of their heated guard shack to check the passenger list.

Ryan looked at his watch—9:02 am. He spent nine months stateside after his first tour in the Middle East. It was 39 hours since leaving the US behind when he swallowed his last bite of Aunt Morgan's apple crisp. Now only distant memories of flaky pie crust, cinnamon, and tart apples remained—the miles, weather, and time zone changes left a dry taste in his mouth.

Ryan was done with being the platoon's sniper, awarded sergeant's stripes in recognition of his unit's efficient and deadly skirmishes with the Taliban during his first tour. His spotter confirmed all 23 of Ryan's kills, each one a Russell Stevens, whether the man carried an AK-47 and had a towel wrapped around his head or not. He still hadn't killed Russell enough times. Russell Steven's pending trial in Kalamazoo for murdering Ryan's parents was mired in lawyers' countless delays but no matter what, Russell Stevens wouldn't get the death penalty. Michigan took it off their books in 1847. That wasn't right.

While first-tour Marines on the bus bound for the 3rd Battalion of the 4th Marines at FOB Delaram talked about "kicking ass and taking names," Ryan reached into his left breast pocket of his camo jacket and took out a photo of his parents. They were camping in Michigan's Upper Peninsula on Brevort Lake—Mother by the campfire managing a cast-iron skillet, Dad holding up a string of 12-inch trout, smiles as big as the sky. Ryan recalled how thick the fireflies were at dusk that day and a few posed in the air besides his parents in the picture.

He put the photo away. He had new family now—the Marines. As a unit, they were trained to protect each other's flanks, whether on patrol in deserts, mountain passes, or in bars picking up women. Brothers. Ryan never had a brother. He liked having so many.

The bus groaned to a stop in front of the command center where everyone checked in. FOB Delaram was in the northernmost part of Nimruz Province. Ryan looked it up. Unceasingly hot summers and unbearably cold winters—a half mile above sea level with an ethnic population mix of Pashtuns, Baloch, and Tajik. In the distance, unforgiving mountains ringed the area. Ryan wondered how anyone could live in a place like this—let alone why Marines were here—it didn't look like the place was worth a shit. He put away those questions, a marine didn't have to like a job to do a job.

At check-in, he was given a binder with his unit's crest. As platoon leader, the binder held the files of each of the Marines in his platoon. Ryan was curious to know exactly what strengths his Marines had and what they could overcome.

Let's see what we got here.

The 2nd Lieutenant was in his first command and first tour after receiving his commission and getting his brass. Ryan thumbed through the files—Alabama, Louisiana, Mississippi, Texas, Florida, Georgia—on paper it looked like the South was going to war. The Staff Sergeant was Bartholomew "Buzz" Butcher, a 10-year veteran of three Middle East tours. They also landed Lincoln, a bomb-sniffing German Shepherd, along with his handler. Ryan winced with a memory.

Could've used you last tour.

The base housed 1,000 Marines who were relatively safe within the surrounding walls of brick, barbed wire, and lookout towers. Ryan found his way to his platoon's quarters, a kind of Quonset hut buried in the dirt where the Marines would sleep.

So much for luxury.

The members of his platoon would show up within the next two days, and with being too tired to sleep, he found 2nd LT Thomas Williams and they did a walkabout tour of the base.

From his files, Ryan knew quite a bit about LT Williams—22 years old like him, 198 pounds, five-foot-nine, left handed, college grad, ROTC, married two months ago to Gretchen from Coral Gables, Florida. *A silver spoon girl.* Far from athletic with a noticeable tire around his waist, Ryan wondered how he ever made it through OCS.

They asked around and found the base's two highlights—poking their heads inside the well-equipped sweaty gym, then heading over to the internet café with its bank of computers.

"Got to keep in touch with my wife. You know, Turner, I just got married," LT Williams said winking and tapped his silver wedding band. "Bet you got a girl and family to talk to back home. Uh, where you from anyway, Turner?"

"Kalamazoo. And no, no girlfriend, Sir." Ryan changed the subject. "Hey, let's check out mess and see if we're not too late for breakfast."

On their walk over to the mess hall, LT Williams told Ryan, "You know, Turner, the root of the word 'mess' is from old French m-e-s meaning 'portion of food.'" LT Williams tried too hard to connect with Ryan. He even bent slightly like he was a waiter serving hors d'oeuvres.

So, that's what you learned at OCS.

Ryan gave a little smile. "Good to know, Sir."

Mess accommodated them even though it was nearer to lunch than breakfast. The cooks knew when buses entered the base with Marine replacements and were always ready. Scrambled eggs, crisp bacon, toast, oatmeal, and gallons of coffee were the bill of fare.

"So, this is your second tour, right, Turner?" LT Williams leaned in, not wanting to let anyone hear. He nervously stirred a mound of cream and sugar into his coffee and waited for Ryan.

"Yes, Sir. I worked out of Camp Rhino and went on patrols to just about everywhere during my nine months." Ryan shoveled in a spoonful of oatmeal, making sure he got an elusive lump of brown sugar in the mix.

"I saw your file. I mean, as your commanding officer, I have the right to review the men in my command," he explained. "You were. I mean, you had…" LT Williams drummed his fork, awkward in what he really wanted to ask.

Ryan knew. "I was our unit's sniper." He waited for the lieutenant's next question.

"What's it like, Turner, you know—I mean, to kill someone?" He stopped drumming his fork.

"Well, it's easier when you're holding an M40 and looking through a high-powered scope from a thousand yards away. Much different than hunting moose or elk. I told myself I needed to do my job well or men in my unit would die." Ryan pushed away his plate, the memories taking away his appetite. "Think I'll head back and crash for a few hours—if that's alright with you, Sir."

"Twenty-three kills," LT Williams shook his head. "Whew."

Ryan kept a stoic face.

"No problem, Turner. Anyway, I need to check in with Major Oaks, our CO."

They both stood, and for the briefest of moments Ryan couldn't tell whether LT Williams wanted to salute or shake hands. Instead, LT Williams nodded and headed out of mess through a back flap.

***

Two days later, the 43 members of their platoon were fully assembled under one roof. Right away, Staff Sergeant Buzz Butcher and Platoon Sergeant Ryan Turner put together a tight schedule to keep their rifle platoon busy with exercises, drills, basics, and familiarizing them on local customs. They even learned a few Pashto phrases—"stop," "on the ground," and "put down your weapon."

During breaks in their training, when they asked if there were any questions, a young Marine asked, "Why can't we just say, "Up against the wall, motherfucker?""

We got a loose group. Nice.

Ryan and Buzz went through the exercises and drills with their platoon, sweating alongside them. Ryan gained 20 pounds of muscle since joining the Marines and they were spread across his six-foot-two-inch frame. The two sergeants overheard comments like, "How the fuck are they not tired?" from the young Marines. That made Buzz and Ryan smile.

Buzz looked like his name—the way a 29-year-old Marine veteran should—high and tight haircut, a jaw that could cut steel, and scars that spoke of more than the tours of duty he completed and the ribbons he wore. He rolled his own cigarettes faster than most people could take one out of a pack.

LT Williams briefed Ryan and Buzz about an upcoming operation where a squad of 16 hand-picked Marines from their platoon would provide cover for another platoon tasked with clearing houses in Washir, a city with suspected Taliban strongholds. Buzz would take them out and head one section of eight, Ryan leading the other eight Marines. The new let's-kick-ass-and-take-names Marines weren't in that mindset anymore—Buzz made sure of that.

"Follow our commands and don't hesitate," Buzz barked. "We're providing cover and watching their asses. But that can change in a second if some motherfuckin' Taliban decides to attack or put up resistance. Got that?"

"Yes, Staff Sergeant," they yelled in unison.

You got 'em where we need 'em.

***

The operation was intense but without incident, lasting seven hours. The 16 Marines in their platoon helicoptered back to base dragging their heels. They headed straight to mess, took showers, then hit the rack. Ryan thought back on the day as he wrote up his report. He was proud of them.

We moved well as a unit. No mistakes. No one lagged. Tight. Now, time to train the other 27 for combat ... because it's coming.

8

RYAN

By the time five months passed into Ryan's second tour, he and Buzz had their platoon of 43 Marines molded into a tight operational unit. They took the lead in over twenty operations and fought in a dozen engagements, feeling the toll from each one of them. Every Marine found their own way to blow off steam and decompress from the action. Some pumped iron. Other played video games, played cards, or jumped online to Skype with their loved ones back home. Ryan's antidote was music, anything by the Eagles—*Take it Easy* his favorite.

The notes Ryan wrote up for their three casualties were hard. Writing "brave" or "fearless" didn't capture what these men meant to him, but what he wrote would most likely end up in the colonel's DD Form 1300 and sent to the next of kin, so his words mattered. He couldn't say that the men were taken out by snipers—the bullets arriving well before the sound of the shot. His platoon got the snipers but not before four other Marines were wounded. Those were the hard—no, impossible moments to put behind him.

***

Ryan, Buzz, and LT Williams met in Captain Oak's tent at zero nine-thirty for briefing on their next mission.

"We got good intel on a band of twenty-two Taliban, light infantry, making their way out of Gulistan and headed west in the next three days. We presume they'll hook up with a larger contingent near Dizak," Captain Oaks said, pointing to a map sprawled across two tables. He chomped on a stubby unlit cigar. "You'll set up west of their location, about sixty klicks from here outside a small village that doesn't show on the map. Your job is to dissuade the Taliban from advancing."

Ryan nodded. *Dissuade? I hear Ivy League.*

"Will we have any support should we run into heavy resistance?" LT Williams asked.

You know the right questions to ask now.

"You'll have active satellite feeds via radio contact, and if need be, we can scramble choppers—but that may take an hour or two." Captain Oaks looked at his watch.

LT Williams winced. "So, basically we're on our own for three days."

"If things get hot, and I don't have any reason to think the will—these Taliban, when they see over forty Marines, tend to run the other way—radio your location and we'll get on it." Captain Oaks looked at each of the men. "Standard ROE remains in effect. If they fire on you, unleash hell. Until then, remain defensive. Make sure your men have full winter camouflage gear and enough ordnance—just in case." He paused and looked them over. "Butcher, Turner, any questions?"

"No, Sir," the said in unison.

***

Ryan and Buzz's squad leaders spent the afternoon making sure each Marine in their unit got their Deuce Gear right: body armor; seven 30-round mags for their M-14s; .45-cal Colt 1911 with two magazines; an IFAK, although they had a Navy corpsman; camelback water bladder; flashlight; NODs; four grenades; iodine tablets and filtration straws; two-man tents; and, a rucksack filled with rations and other gear. It was over 70 pounds. They slapped fresh batteries into helmet comms, flashlights, NODs, and anything else requiring power.

Ryan and Buzz looked at the men with pride, arms folded across their chests, wide stance—barking out reminders of what some Marines were missing. The supply sergeant stood at the end of their Quonset hut busy filling their requests. When their gear was all spread out on the deck, it didn't look like any normal human could carry it all, but they weren't normal—they were Marines.

Ryan recalled strapping on the 70-plus pounds of gear during his first Afghan deployment. He was all of 180 pounds back then and it took some effort to adjust to the weight across his six-foot two-inch frame. With an added 25 pounds of muscle a year later, now the 70 pounds hardly made a dent in his stride.

Guys traded their rations for what they liked—some focused on the tortellini, and the heat-em-up pouches, others the MRE's version of pop tarts. It sounded like a bazaar with pouches and packages flying all around the barracks. Ryan got a kick out of the gum that was included—a laxative because the MREs were designed to constipate Marines, limiting vulnerable situations in the field.

After mess at 1800, Ryan, Buzz, and LT Williams brought their platoon together—to go over the mission, ROE, communications, weather, and the topography of the land where they'd be *dissuading* the Taliban.

***

"We'll helo out at 0400," LT Williams concluded. "We have rations for three days but hope to wrap up this op in two. Weather this time of year is sub-freezing, so wear your white cammies and break out your thermals. Any final questions?"

Nuñez, the joker in their unit and their shortest Marine, raised his hand.

LT Williams answered rolling his eyes. "Yes, Nuñez."

"Well, Sir, since tomorrow is Valentine's Day and it's going to be cold as hell, any chance of me going stateside to get Lupita? She knows how to keep me real warm."

A few Marines let out hoots followed by, "Three hundred pounds of love," and "Oh, does your mamacita have a sister?"

"Chow at 0300, so get some shut-eye," Buzz called out, a roll-your-own ready to light up. "Dismissed."

***

They brought along Lincoln, their bomb sniffing German Shepherd and his handler, Ramirez, lanky and bearded. It was unusual because they didn't expect to be doing any house-to-house clearing, but Lincoln could smell Taliban long before anyone saw them. Andrews, a big southern boy from Alabama, was their radioman and would stay in touch with command—an extra 20 pounds of equipment for him to handle. Daniels, a chubby first-tour Navy corpsman from Arkansas, was the platoon's medic, although each of the men carried an IFAK strapped to their lower backs.

They lifted off at 0400 as planned and were inserted at 0505. Ryan looked up. It was eerie watching the four choppers disappear into the darkness, the whirr of their blades fading into the early morning, dust swirling around them.

Twenty degrees on the ground. That woke up everyone. A burp of the warm eggs, bacon, hash browns, and hot coffee at chow reminded him they would see that in a couple of days.

They moved out using hand signals and person-to-person radio commands coming mostly from Buzz and Ryan. Using their NODs to see in the dark, they set up their two-man tents across a quarter-mile of winding dry wash, about 40 yards separating each facing the village. Stationed 50 yards west of the *dissuasion* line were eight other two-man tents to cover the backside and flanks—just in case.

The radioman, corpsman, and Lincoln and his handler were stationed near the middle of the line facing the village with LT Williams. Buzz was centered on the left flank, Ryan to the right, squad leaders scattered about. It was 0630 before they were in place and their position was secure.

The terrain was hilly and winding so visual contact wasn't possible for everyone in the platoon, but a friendly voice was just a whisper away with their personal comms. Ryan shared a tent with Nuñez and his stories of Lupita's sexual antics kept him amused. At dawn, they put away their night-vision goggles that were trained on the small goat village.

Ryan checked on each of his paired Marines and made his way back to LT Williams where he and Buzz were to get an update on their mission.

"Command says there's a front coming through just north of us around 0200 tomorrow that shouldn't give us some flurries," LT Williams said as he stood stomping his feet to keep the circulation going. "The Taliban are still on course to arrive here in a day or so. Weather wise, we should be all right. Turner, how's everything on your line?"

Buzz took out a pre-rolled cigarette and nodded to Ryan, who took the queue. "All's quiet on my southwestern front, Sir."

"And you, Butcher?"

Buzz exhaled into the cold air. "Same here, Sir."

"Well, let's just wait then." LT Williams shrugged. "As discussed, let's do a physical check on the men every four hours and then report to me in person. Anything to add?"

Both Ryan and Buzz shook their heads and strode off to be with their men.

The day continued much the same, the most excitement being a pregnant goat wandering into the dry wash late in the day and then taking off towards the village when someone rang a dinner bell.

***

Like clockwork, the temperature dropped to zero and snow flurries began at 0200, each of the Marines zipping up their tents, leaving enough room for one of them to keep eyes on the distance with their NODs. Ryan received a comm from LT Williams just after 0500, Buzz on the call as well.

"Butcher, Turner—command's latest is that the weather's changed. Storm's headed south right through our location. We're going to see some heavy snow."

That means cloud cover and no intel on enemy movements.

"Latest—the Taliban is still a day out and headed in our direction. Let's recon at 0800."

"Yes, Sir," Ryan and Buzz said in unison.

Fucking weather.

***

Three hours later, Ryan and Buzz stood with LT Williams with their backs to a driving snow, the kind that's so cold it doesn't stick to anything except exposed skin. "Command has this storm gaining strength but I think we can wait it out. Any thoughts?"

"Taliban's got to deal with the same shit, Sir," Ryan said rubbing his gloves together.

"It'd be shame to bring us all the way out here to dance with some Taliban just to go back to base because of a few snowflakes, Sir," Buzz said, his grim face saying he was ready for action despite the chill.

"Well, see you at noon," LT Williams grumbled.

***

The snow fell all day—quiet—and steady. It reminded Ryan of hunting elk with his father in northern Michigan. The simple pleasures of stalking game, quiet hand signals, staying down wind, waiting for the sound of a twig snapping.

Don't think about that right now.

Every four hours when they checked in with LT Williams, it was the same. Cloud cover inhibited satellite intel to tell them of any ground movements and the weather looked as if could get worse.

Three hours after sunset, the weather turned into a blinding snowstorm with 40 mile-per-hour howling winds, the snow surging sideways. Ryan scurried between his two-man tents with the message of, "Hunker down. It's going to be a long one."

***

Ryan stepped out of his tent at dawn, the sun hiding behind thick clouds. Snow drifts as high as two feet sprouted up anywhere there was an outcropping. Their two-man white camouflage tents looked like large bleached turtle shells dotted across the landscape. Ryan waded through light snow to check on each of his men, then headed toward LT Williams' tent where Buzz also waited.

"I thought Kalamazoo was cold, but this, this is fu-fu-fucking cold," Ryan said, mimicking a stutter.

"Michigan or Michigan State?" Buzz asked brushing snow from his dark eyebrows.

"Really? Eastern Michigan Eagles, who else?" Ryan laughed.

LT Williams popped out of his tent. "Miami Hurricanes for me," he said looking up into the gray sky and swirling snow. "Could use some tropical weather right about now."

"What's the outlook, Sir?" Ryan asked.

"Turner, same shit, different day," LT Williams answered. "Command's thinking of canceling the op. They've got no eyes to tell us what the Taliban's doing. They might fly in a supply drop—but not in this weather."

Buzz grumbled. "Rotorheads afraid their windshields will ice up, Sir?"

"Yeah, Butcher," LT Williams answered. "Let's keep with the same four-hour check-in. Anything pops, I'll let you know."

Nothing happened during the night but more snow.

***

At 0650 things popped. Lincoln growled, Ramirez alerted LT Williams. "Lincoln picked up something—and it ain't goats."

LT Williams passed along the word to Ryan and Buzz and they let their men know. Tents unzipped letting in the frigid air. Caps on scopes popped off—eyes fixed on the village. They waited. Half an hour. An hour. Nothing.

It was getting light. LT instructed the platoon to go to one man on watch while the other grabbed some MREs or took a morning piss.

Buzz and Ryan checked on everyone and they made their way back to the center of the line for an update with the LT. With nothing of substance to relay—command said to sit tight. As LT wandered off a few steps into the wash to take a piss in the snow, a Lee-Enfield .303 slug struck the middle of his face, his helmet flying off, some of the splatter from his brain hitting Ryan.

"Shot fired! Sniper! West of us!" Ryan yelled into his comm.

Everyone hit the deck.

"Corpsman! Second LT down!" Ryan barked.

Buzz, next in command, hand-signaled Ryan he was headed towards Andrews to radio in their engagement, taking cover where he could.

The corpsman came from behind Ryan and crawled quickly toward the LT while Ryan searched the terrain across from their location. Quiet tension—the kind just before a shit storm. He glanced at Daniels who felt for LT Williams' pulse. Seconds later, Daniels looked to Ryan and shook his head.

Ryan's first tour as a sniper taught him the shooter would most likely be camouflaged in thick brush or blended into a fallen tree, the only thing protruding would be the barrel of his rifle. No movement. No reflection. No color. No sound.

Two of the tents west of Ryan, across the wash, were strafed by machine gun fire, Ryan catching the flash of AK-47s.

"I got 'em, Buzz!" Ryan shouted into his comm.

"Where?"

"West of me, on the ridge above the wash. Maybe 100 yards out. They took out two of our tents. Corpsman!"

"Engage those motherfuckers!" Buzz commanded.

9

KENNEDY

The drill was always the same—lie there and take it. She didn't participate when it came to sex, except for her moans of discomfort, which he took as passion. Lie there and take it. That's exactly what she did. Kennedy lived her life like that for the first six months of their marriage. Wake up, make him breakfast, keep a spotless house, prepare his dinner, and when he came home—lie there and take it—or sometimes bend over and take it.

He eventually got around to blaming her half-breed heritage on why she wasn't pregnant yet. "They're half-drunk or on peyote most of the time. You better not have taken any of those drugs."

"I didn't, Logan. I told you that." She lowered her voice. "And they're not all like that."

"You need to get to a doctor and find out what's wrong with you. And if it's—well, we'll figure out what I need to do when you find out."

***

After Kennedy's OB/Gyn couldn't find any problems with her, he referred her to a fertility specialist. Following her second visit to the specialist, she walked into her office cautiously, almost tiptoeing in and taking a seat.

"First of all, you can take a deep breath. Everything's fine," Dr. Donna Graham said, her short brown hair and glasses giving her an air of professionalism. She paused to gauge Kennedy's reaction. "You have healthy eggs, no deviations in your pelvic area or uterus, your tubes are perfectly shaped, and you have the ideal hormone balance. Even if things are perfect, it takes some couples years before they conceive."

Kennedy stared at her blankly, the thought of unending vicious sex with Logan filling her head.

Years?

Dr. Graham continued, "We should test your husband. It's not uncommon for college athletes to experience low sperm count if they've experienced certain injuries."

Kennedy shook her head emphatically. "He'll never do that."

"You've been to see me twice, Kennedy. How important is it to find out why you're not getting pregnant?"

Kennedy squirmed in her seat. "I—I can't ask him…" her voice trailed off.

Doctor Graham gave a knowing nod. "We're used to working with those *situations*. Some men are like that. Let me make a suggestion."

***

It was three days since they had sex, Logan fighting off a nasty cold. Kennedy wouldn't wish sickness like that on anyone, but it was a wonderful break. He woke early Friday proud of his morning wood and eager to put it to work. He rarely kissed her or did any foreplay when they had sex and this was no different. She lay there moaning because of the pain until he finished with his usual grunt, rolled off of her, and without a word, headed to the shower.

Kennedy snuck into their second bathroom, took out the kit Dr. Graham gave her, and squatted over the collection cup for a few minutes. She texted the doctor's office and received a message back to get the sample to them as soon as possible.

She fixed Logan a light breakfast and his special coffee, ushering him out the door.

***

She sat in the waiting room—and waited. The parade of women coming in for tests, hormone treatments, and operations—all to have a baby—was stunning. So many.

Do your husbands have sex with you the same as mine?

She was interrupted by the receptionist and escorted into Dr. Graham's office. The tests confirmed her worse fear—no matter how many times they had sex, she couldn't get pregnant. Logan was sterile.

How do I tell him?

Kennedy broke down in uncontrollable sobs.

Dr. Graham came around the desk and sat next to Kennedy placing an arm around her shoulder. After Kennedy calmed down, the doctor offered, "In instances like this, you have a number of options." She paused until she got a nod from Kennedy to continue. "There's always adoption."

Kennedy shook her head violently. "Logan would *never* agree to that."

"We could use a donor."

Kennedy crinkled her face in disgust. "You mean have sex with another man?"

"No, no." Dr. Graham smiled. "We have access to a nationwide sperm bank with details about the donors—everything from their DNA which includes the color of their hair and eyes, height, family history, and IQ. The procedure is called in vitro fertilization, a minor technique that takes a couple of visits. Does that sound like an option?"

Kennedy grabbed a tissue off the desk, blew her nose, wiped her eyes, and sat up with a sense of purpose. "How long will it take? And what will it cost?" She paused and took a deep breath. "And does my husband need to know?"

***

Three months later, Logan found Kennedy waiting for him by the door when he got home from work. Something strange was in her eyes, a sparkle, a playfulness—and she wore a new short black dress with heels, her hair put up, wedding jewelry adorning her neck, ears, and wrists.

"What? What is it, Kennedy?"

She said nothing but took his hand and led him to the outdoor patio. There were candles everywhere and what looked to be an elegant meal already prepared—sterling silver domes covering their plates. Andrea Bocelli filled the air from hidden Bose speakers.

"Did I forget something." He looked at his Rolex. "Did I miss a special date again?" Logan pressed.

"No, silly. Why don't you sit down? I spent all afternoon fixing this."

They sat across from each other, Kennedy the most alive Logan had seen since they were married.

She stared into his eyes. "I lied," she said playfully and flipped her bangs.

"About what?" he asked leaning forward.

"I've been working on this longer than this afternoon. If I had to guess, it's been 10 months in the making."

Logan scrunched his forehead and tilted his head to the side in confusion.

"Let's eat and I'll tell you all about it." She grabbed the lid of her dome and motioned Logan to do the same. "On three. One. Two. Three."

They lifted the sterling silver covers off their plates. Confusion hit Logan when he looked down at a six-inch by ½-inch piece of beige plastic in the middle of a Royal Worchester dinner plate. He glanced at Kennedy's plate and spotted vitamins.

"Turn it over," Kennedy said, brimming with excitement.

"I don't—"

"Just turn it over and look," she commanded.

Logan picked up the plastic and turned it over. It took a few seconds for it to register—then he looked up with tears in his eyes. "I'm going to be a father?"

Their smiles met—the most intimate moment they ever shared.

They drove, or raced as Kennedy called it, to Fleming's Steakhouse, their favorite restaurant. Kennedy as usual cautioned Logan to slow down and not weave between cars.

"Please. You're driving for three now," she said.

He slowed for a few blocks, then he was back to his old habits.

He called his mother to share the news. When she answered the phone, he blurted out, "Guess what?"

By the excitement in his voice she knew. "She's finally pregnant?"

You make it sound like I'm only a baby maker—I have a name.

"We won't know the gender for a few months," Kennedy said. "We're on our way to Flemings to celebrate."

"Oh, hello, Kennedy," Linda Young said more warmly than normal. "You must be excited. We've got lots of planning to do before the arrival of my grandchild. I can't wait to pick out everything for the nursery. The baby shower will be so much fun. And you're going to need a proper home with a backyard, not your penthouse condo. The due date is going—oh, we'll get to that later. I'll contact Rob, my real estate agent, first thing—heck, I'll call him right now. Ciao!"

She hung up and Logan reached over and squeezed Kennedy's hand. "She's a little excited, don't you think?" He winked at her.

Kennedy hadn't seen this playful side of him since they first started dating and she beamed back at him and squeezed his hand in return.

At the restaurant, Logan pulled out the chair for Kennedy and doted on her, like when the waiter asked if she wanted her usual Opus One Pinot Noir.

"Not for the next eight months," Logan said. He paused while the waiter took it in. When he saw the recognition flicker in the eyes, he said, "That's right, we're having a baby!"

That night Logan shared his good fortune with anyone who would listen. He eventually turned off his phone due to the constant texts and phone calls—the long reach of Linda Young's voice stirring up the gossip pot already.

As always, he drank too much, so Kennedy insisted she drive home. She was apprehensive not only because he was so reckless on the road but because she knew what would happen to her when he drank. This time he didn't attack her when they got home. Instead, he passed out on their bed.

Kennedy took off his shoes and pulled a blanket over him. She looked down at him—*peaceful* was the word that popped into her head.

Maybe you'll be different because of the baby.

***

Everything changed at 5:06 am Sunday. The red LED clock on her night stand pulsed out the large numbers when Kennedy blinked her eyes open and reached for her ringing cell phone.

Linda Young's anguished voice cut through the early morning darkness. "He's gone," she gasped.

Kennedy switched on a lamp and looked over at Logan's empty side of the bed. She asked a cautious, "Who? What?"

"Logan. My Logan is gone," she tried to control her sobs.

"No. He's playing poker with his friends, that's all. He just hasn't come home yet," Kennedy whispered.

"I'm at the morgue now—to—to identify his body."

After that, Kennedy couldn't make out a word she said. Death was a natural occurrence on the reservation, she saw it up close during the ten years she lived there. The universal message was that life is temporary, we're just passing through, and we hope to leave the earth a better place than when we arrived—but it was different when it happened to you.

She called the police to get the address for the Medical Examiner's office. She knew she was in no condition to drive to the Kearney Mesa area. Kennedy called Uber to drive her the 12.6 miles to view her dead husband's body. It took them 31 minutes.

***

Logan's Porsche did its best to keep him safe, but without him wearing a seatbelt he hardly stood a chance. He lost control of the SUV and rolled down a foggy ravine off Torrey Pines Road. His face was crushed and lacerated to the point of being unrecognizable but Linda insisted on an open casket ceremony—and when Linda demanded something with her checkbook open, it happened.

Except for the casket and Kennedy dressed in black, it was hard to tell it was a funeral, Linda Young pulling out all the stops with a celebrity-studded event. The same faces that were at the wedding, who gave such lavish gifts, were somber and quiet with their condolences.

More than once, Kennedy overheard Linda say, "At least I'll have my grandchild to remember him by. Oh, and of course, his mother, who Logan loved so much." Air kisses and empty hugs accompanied every solemn hello and goodbye.

The service was tasteful with its pageantry, somewhere between a US Senator's memorial and a city major's. An opera singer from the symphony sang Ave Maria that had everyone bowing their heads and weeping.

Kennedy only said a few words. Like her wedding day, everything was a blur—with too much to remember and so much to forget.

***

One thing good about Logan was that he was prepared. A million-dollar life insurance policy and mortgage insurance meant Kennedy wouldn't have to worry about money for quite some time.

In the months that followed until the baby was born, Linda Young invaded every aspect of Kennedy's life. Carpenters and painters came over and turn Logan's penthouse apartment office into a nursery. Then she filled it with every conceivable high-end prop Kennedy would need to fulfill her role as mother to Linda's grandson.

"Are you getting enough sleep? Is the nutrition from what you're eating and those vitamins enough? Maybe we should get you a nutritionist. Should you be exercising so much in your condition? I hear Yoga's not good for you." Linda shared her opinions freely and demanded answers.

A month before the baby was due, Linda insisted Kennedy come to her place for dinner. "It'll be quiet with no distractions," she said.

Kennedy put her long dark hair in a single braid and found herself chewing on the end of it, an old habit from when she was young. The baby kicked and she smiled.

"A month more, Easton," she whispered and rubbed her belly.

You already discussed the name, his religious upbringing, and what would happen should I remarry. But what happens when you find out Logan is not Easton's father?

***

Before they started on their salads, she sensed Linda about to explode, nervously tapping her fork on the edge of her plate and looking down at her cell phone.

"Expecting a call?" Kennedy asked.

Linda looked up, her face full of concern and doubt. Her normal Pilates-toned body slumped slightly and her fake suntan and makeup couldn't hide she didn't get much sleep. "No. No, I have a few notes. I want to get this right."

"That never stopped you before," Kennedy joked

Linda returned a thin smile. "I spoke with my lawyers and they've put something together for me—for us." She cleared her throat, took a sip of water, and looked at her notes. "This is kind of unusual, but not out of the question. It's been done before—so there's precedence." She paused to see how Kennedy would react.

What are you up to now?

"You sound just like a lawyer," Kennedy said and smiled.

Linda didn't return the smile. "I thought we could talk about having a pre-birth agreement, you know, like the prenup you had with Logan. Only this one involves the baby."

Kennedy's face flushed in anger and confusion. "What?" she asked.

"I was thinking, with all you've been through, that maybe the care for Logan's child might become too much for you, even overwhelming with—"

"His name is Easton," Kennedy interrupted, her teeth clenched.

Linda fought to keep her composure, gritting her teeth. "I know how much you loved Logan. Think of him now. He provided for you—a home that's paid off—life and health insurance. Heaven forbid something unfortunate should happen to you, and I don't expect it to—but should that happen, I would take over guardianship of my grandson, and compensate you for your..." her voice faded along with her confidence as Kennedy's mouth hung open in disbelief.

Kennedy clutched her swollen belly and pushed herself away from the table. "I stood by and let you redecorate everything the way you wanted. I switched doctors because you insisted I have the best in all of San Diego. You've controlled every aspect of my pregnancy. And now, you don't even believe I'll make a good mother—to Easton. You can't even say his name. You're ridiculous!" Kennedy stood, grabbed her purse, and headed for the door. "I'm done with you."

"Don't you even want to know how much?" Linda yelled after Kennedy.

Kennedy stopped at the front door and whirled around. "No amount of money can buy my baby. And just so you know, Logan wasn't the same man you and your friends made speeches about at his funeral. He was cruel, self-centered, and didn't respect his wife. I'm glad he's dead. I wouldn't want him raising Easton."

Linda's mouth hung open as Kennedy swung the door open and slammed it shut.

10

KENNEDY

U nder threat of legal action, Kennedy mended fences with Linda a few weeks before the birth of Easton. It was the most difficult meeting she ever attended—three-piece-suit lawyers sitting across the table with a court stenographer typing away, recording Kennedy's every word. Kennedy smiled and made nice, even signing Linda's pre-birth agreement, giving her custody should anything happen to Kennedy or should she be unable to care for Easton.

Five million dollars. That's what you think my love for Easton is worth?

When she left the lawyers' office, Kennedy made a vow to herself. *When my son is old enough, I'll take him away from you, and you'll never see him again.*

***

Kennedy's labor lasted three hours and the delivery was trouble-free—six months of yoga classes preparing the birth canal. As expected, Linda was at the hospital, hovering outside the delivery room, making sure Aruna, the famous doula she flew in from India, did her job to attend to the mother and baby during the delivery. Aruna hummed soothing chants while she dabbed Valerian calming oil on Kennedy's forehead and wrists.

Eight pounds, four ounces. Blond-hair, blue-eyes, chubby cheeks and thick legs, and the smallest toes. Kennedy couldn't take her eyes off Easton as he rested against her chest—small breaths matching hers with sweet contented coos coming from his perfect pink lips.

I'm in love.

As soon as Kennedy's delivery was over, a photographer and stylist appeared. Linda hired them to capture the new mother and child in all their glory.

"It's a momentous occasion," Linda declared circling Kennedy's bed as she instructed the stylist and photographer. "My first, and probably, what am I talking about … my only grandchild."

As tired as she was, Kennedy posed for pictures with Easton and his grandmother.

Linda looked over the shoulder of the photographer at a digital picture on the camera's back and winced. "My word. It's horrible my grandson doesn't have teeth. Can you add some when you make the prints?" she asked the photographer.

The photographer glanced at the stylist and tried to hide his shock. "Why, yes, we can do that, Mrs. Young. You're the first person ever to request that." He made it sound like she invented something new, like the cure for cancer.

Kennedy was glad when Aruna shooed everyone out of the room, her thick Indian accent making the harsh words seem kind. "You go now. Baby and mother need rest if milk is to come."

***

Aruna moved into Kennedy's condo to provide help with breastfeeding as well as an extra set of loving hands. At barely five feet tall and thin, Aruna greeted Kennedy and Easton each morning with quiet smiles and a fresh red dot in her forehead. She bowed slightly with her hands together in prayer, her bright billowing sari almost making her look like an angel. "You and baby are so radiant, full of life."

Aruna's humble and wise ways were a gift to Kennedy. She was so unlike other people she met since moving to San Diego with her mother when she was ten. She reminded Kennedy of Miss Betty Old Horn.

I need to contact her.

Aruna guided Kennedy in the simple things, like changing the baby's diaper or preparing her nipples for nursing. She and Easton were always met with a kindness and a gentleness Kennedy never experienced since her mother passed away.

"Even though he cannot speak, your baby will tell you if his stomach is upset, if he needs his diaper changed, if he is hungry, has an ear ache—or if he feels lonely. You must listen to his energy, feel his chakras."

Kennedy's forehead wrinkled. "Chakras?"

Aruna took Kennedy's hand and placed it over Easton's small body. "Close your eyes and feel the energy coming from him—at the base of his spine."

Kennedy looked down at Easton and closed her eyes.

"The first chakra. The root chakra, is his connection to the physical world—the Earth. Bright red color signifies he feels safe and things are as they are meant to be. Do you feel it? Do you see it?" Aruna hummed a deep tone. "This sound belongs to the first chakra."

A warm red glow filled Kennedy's mind and she felt a vibration coming from Easton, a vibration that matched Aruna's humming. "Yes. Yes, I do." When she opened her eyes, the connection was lost. She turned to Aruna. "Is this how you can tell what Easton needs?"

Aruna smiled and nodded her head. "Now, close your eyes and let's feel the second chakra."

Each day Kennedy practiced reading Easton's seven chakras. She was amazed she could tell what was going on inside Easton, sometimes his first red chakra dimmed. Those times she would hold him close, and in her warmth and safety he would calm and his chakra would again turn bright red. This nudged memories out of Kennedy—of her life on the Crow reservation when she was young with Miss Betty Old Horn and her spiritual ways.

"Aruna, is there some kind of connection between what you believe in India and the Native Americans?"

Aruna cocked her head to one side. "I do not understand your American Indians but this I know, we are all creatures of God meant to live in a physical world but we remain in touch with our creator through nature. If this is what your natives believe, then, yes."

"I always thought so." Kennedy looked down at Easton and saw a red glow emanating from the base of his spine. Her mouth hung open. "I can see it with my eyes open."

Aruna gave her a warm hug. "You are close to your child in a way that is meant to be."

"I can't wait to tell Linda."

Aruna shook her head slowly. "I do not think it wise. Miss Linda is not open to the spiritual world. Yes, she hired me, but her heart is clouded by the death of her husband and son—and her need for power. She is not open to the spiritual world."

You're probably right.

That night, Kennedy began to plan for the day she and Easton would leave Linda's grasp. It took her two hours to write what she wanted to say in a letter to Miss Betty Old Horn, her Crow grandmother. It was simple. This would be the last time Kennedy would contact her—until she saw her on the reservation. Miss Betty Old Horn would know when Kennedy and Easton would arrive. She ended the letter with, "You will feel our spirits coming to you."

***

Kennedy did the math. Nine thousand, nine-hundred dollars a week over two years. The transactions had to be under $10,000 so as not to alert the IRS and call attention to what she was doing. One hundred weeks. One million dollars from Logan's life insurance. Cashier's checks using a variety of banks and money orders from the post office would hide her trail.

She had to be careful—their lives depended on it.

***

Kennedy, Easton, and Aruna created a pleasant rhythm— daily walks in the morning and evening, a weekly visit to the Birch Aquarium, and watching the seals at the children's pool. Easton's eyes would sparkle with delight and his chubby arms would reach out when he came in touch with nature's wonders.

I wonder if his sperm donor was like this.

Each day, at exactly one in the afternoon, Linda's chauffeur would drop her off to spend precisely an hour with Easton. She always brought age-inappropriate gifts, assuming he could do more—like a motorized tricycle when he was two months old. "He'll be riding it in no time," she said with the confidence of a wealthy, clueless, doting grandmother. "Even Logan wasn't this far along at this stage. My, but he takes after him."

Aruna would take the hour during Linda's visits to spend time on the deck of Kennedy's penthouse doing kundalini yoga.

Linda smirked. "What's with all her stretching and holding poses? It doesn't look like exercise to me. Is she looking after you and Easton properly? You know, I can get someone else if you'd like." Linda's perpetual frown punctuated her lack of understanding.

"No, Aruna's remarkable. She's taught me things that…" Kennedy looked out to the deck and paused to collect her thoughts, careful to choose the right words. "She taught me things you can't find in books—about connecting with Easton to understand him when he can't talk yet."

"Just wait until he does talk. You'll get an earful. Logan was like that…" A sadness fell over Linda's face for a few moments, then she looked at her watch. "Darrell's waiting downstairs for me in the car." She woke up Easton when she tickled him with her perfectly polished nails. "We make a beautiful little family, don't we?"

She stood and picked up her purse, gave Kennedy an air kiss, and was off to the front door. "Don't worry, I'll let myself out," she said with her back to Kennedy.

***

Easton's two bottom front teeth came at four months and then his top two front teeth two months later.

"He's going to be something," Aruna said while changing his diaper. "Really something. I've seen many babies. When their teeth come early that means they are destined for greatness." She wrapped him in a colorful sari.

The doorbell rang. Aruna looked at Kennedy, a polite smile on her face. "I'll let Miss Linda in."

Later during Linda's visit, as they sipped tea, she broached the subject Kennedy dreaded. "I think it's time for Aruna to leave."

"Really?"

"You don't know how much this is costing me." Linda shook her head as if to disagree with herself. "Not that money is an issue. When it comes to my only grandchild, it means nothing."

Then why bring it up?

Kennedy's eyes pleaded. "Can she stay at least until the month's up?"

"I think that can be arranged. Maybe I'll get you a part-time au pair, someone from France. She can teach Easton another language. Wouldn't that be nice?"

"Linda, I speak another language, the language of my people—Crow."

"Oh that. I meant a real language people will understand and respect."

Kennedy took in the clueless woman and nodded her head, politely smiling.

Linda took Easton's hands in hers. "You'll get a law degree, become a congressman, senator, then…" her voice trailed and she lowered her head. "I only wish Logan could be here to watch you. I hope I'll live to see the day…" Her eyes welled with tears.

Kennedy reached over in comfort and patted Linda's hand in a rare display of physical contact.

Linda pulled her hand back and stood. "I've got to go now." She bent and tickled Easton.

He looked at her with an odd expression of curiosity.

"See, he likes his grandma Linda, don't you?" She tickled him again.

Easton gave her a toothy grin.

"Just like his father!" She picked up her Kate Spade bag and headed out the door.

***

After Kennedy and Aruna finished putting Easton to bed and closed his bedroom door, they retreated to the living room and sat on the sofa. Kennedy asked, "Aruna, tell me more about your family. How could you leave them and come here for so long?"

"We live in a small village—my parents, uncles, aunts, cousins, my children. My dream was always to build a school and take care of the simple needs of my family. With Miss Linda's money, I can now have my dream."

"I'd like to have a dream like that," Kennedy whispered.

"It is in you, waiting for you to call upon it." Aruna clasped her hands together and bowed slightly. She looked around at the opulent penthouse. "When you leave, you will find it."

How do you know?

***

Easton's first birthday was a celebration Kennedy didn't want—but there was no stopping Linda. She insisted Kennedy and Easton spend the night after the party at her estate on the La Jolla cliffs overlooking the Pacific—the same place where Kennedy and Logan were married.

In the morning, with Easton still asleep, Kennedy grabbed a cup of coffee and watched as a throng of workers took down the big top tent. There had been clowns, monkeys, acrobats, a juggler breathing fire—the entertainment was endless. Hundreds of people, who Kennedy met briefly at her wedding or read about in newspapers, filled the tent and let out "oohs" and "aahs" in appreciation of Linda's excess.

Kennedy spotted Linda with a foreman—pointing out damaged areas to her football field-sized lawn. He busied himself scribbling in a notebook and nodding his head.

Kennedy heard Easton's distinct voice. "Ah-chee. Ah-chee."

"Haw-wah." She answered and smiled to herself. The first word Easton learned was "ah-chee," the Crow word for mother. When Linda heard him, she thought it was baby gibberish. She had no idea Kennedy was teaching him another language.

That's not all he'll learn.

11

RYAN

S taff Sergeant Buzz Butcher called into his comms, "Polski. Thompson." Nothing. "Turner, take roll-call."

Ryan called the Marines by name over his comms starting with Anzo and ending with Zwicki. All but four answered "Up"— Christian. Thompson. Polski. Vernon. "We got four down, Buzz."

"Copy that. Sanchez, take your squad northwest and flank 'em—and I'm comin with you," Butch said.

"Aye, Sarge," Sanchez answered.

"Hollins, take your squad and flank from the southwest. I don't want any heroes or crossfire, you got that?" Buzz commanded.

"Aye, Sarge," Hollins said.

"All other eyes and guns half and half, east and west. We need to know how many fuckin' Tally we're up against and where they're coming from. Now move!" Buzz barked. "And Turner, get the corpsman up to those two tents."

"On it, Buzz," Ryan responded.

Ryan grabbed Nuñez and Daniels, the corpsman, and belly crawled through the snow across the wash towards the two tents.

There was little cover—a boulder here, some scrub brush there, or an occasional tree limb left over from a flood.

Snow puffed up nearby with little geysers of sand.

Shit.

Ryan tapped his comms. "Sniper's on us, Buzz. I need suppressive fire."

Within seconds, beautiful bursts from M-14s rolled across the quiet of the wash to somewhere west of them. Ryan, Nuñez, and Daniels scurried up to the first bullet-ridden tent. Nuñez pulled out his Ka-Bar and slashed the tent so Daniels could enter from the back and check on the Marines. Half a minute later, Daniels returned with blood on his hands.

"Vernon and Polski—both KIA," Daniels whispered.

Fuck.

The usual smell of sour death was missing—the cold smothering it. Ryan swallowed hard thinking of Vernon's upcoming wedding and Polski's new baby.

"The other tent's north of here." Crab crawling over the snow, Ryan glanced back at Nuñez and Daniels. "Stay low."

Fifty yards later, they arrived at the second tent—no sniper fire this trip. Again, Nuñez sliced the tent for Daniels to enter. A few seconds later Daniels' head poked out.

"Christian and Thompson—they're alive but gonna need CasEvac soon."

"Stay with 'em and do what you can. I'll call it in." Ryan turned to Nuñez. "You stay here and provide cover for Daniels or give him an extra set of hands—whatever he needs."

"Aye, Sarge," Nuñez said, his face grim, his normal jokes evaporated after the first bullet of the skirmish.

Ryan tapped his comms, updating Buzz on the KIAs and the two injured Marines.

"Andrews, get a helo here for CasEvac! We got two men down," Buzz ordered.

"Aye, Aye—" Andrews answered and let out a low gurgle. Silence.

"Andrews? Andrews!" Buzz yelled. Silence. "Turner, find out what happened to Andrews and get on the radio."

Heavy bursts of machine gun fire to the north caused Ryan to flatten himself in the snow. "On it," Ryan said. He took off across the wash in a crouch to the comms tent, zig-zagging to make it more difficult for the sniper to get him.

It didn't work.

***

Ryan came to, face buried in the snow, and his right leg hurt like hell. He shook his head trying to clear it.

Must've blacked out.

He slowly turned to look at his leg, the snow around his thigh a bright red. He tapped his comms. "I'm hit, Buzz—but I can make it to Andrews."

"Roger. Keep me posted—every two minutes."

A loud explosion flooded Ryan's ears through the comms and he winced. He looked north and saw smoke and dirt erupt into the air.

We're in the shit now.

It was hard going, his right leg useless—he couldn't push off with it. He used his right forearm to pull himself forward, his left leg to push. The sniper occasionally peppered the snow around him. Looking back into the wash, Ryan noticed the trail of blood—his blood—following him. Heavy breath poured from his mouth in gusts of steam as he struggled against the cold and pain.

Motherfucker.

He crawled to the side of the comms tent where he found Andrews—dead—on his back, bled out through a gaping hole in his neck. Ryan got up on his left knee and struggled to take the radio pack off Andrews. His vision blurred and he shook his head.

Stay awake.

He freed the radio from Andrews and looked down at his leg.

Gotta get a tourniquet.

Something hit his chest plate, knocking the wind out of him, and throwing him on the ground. "Ugh," he moaned and pulled himself up on an elbow, tapping his comms. "Buzz. Andrews is KIA. I got the radio." Silence. "Buzz?" Nothing.

Something slammed into his left shoulder hurling him back onto the snow. Pain. Confusion. When he touched his shoulder, it was warm and wet—and the warmth spread.

What's going—

The radio crackled to life. "Uncle Charlie's Cabin. Do you copy?"

Ryan concentrated and reached out to grab the mic. "Turner here. Got three KIAs including LT Williams. We're under Taliban attack from the west and need CasEvac for three, maybe more, and…" his voice weakened. He blinked his eyes, trying to fight off the darkness taking over his mind.

"Roger, Turner. We're scrambling—"

Shouts in Farsi. AK-47s close by blasted the air. It was cold. Getting colder. Someone stood over Ryan yelling angry words in a language he didn't understand.

He caught a glimpse of a large black bird. It looked at him with concerned eyes. It let out a "caw" and hopped off into the distance.

Wind. Howling wind. Deafening wind. Swirling snow.

Ryan let out a deep sigh as everything faded.

So, this is how it ends.

12

RYAN

Loud voices went in and out of focus. Ryan couldn't see to make out anything. *Taliban!* Bursts of AK-47s erupted around him, hot shell casings raining down on his face and chest. He tried to swipe them away and open his eyes but nothing worked. Rough hands grabbed him and dragged him— he moaned. *My leg!* An explosion. The hands released him and he heard the dull thud of a dead man hit the ground next to him. Ryan raised an arm and tried to call out but all he could produce was a faint gurgle. Then dark silence.

***

In flutters, the darkness lifted—like a lazy fat bird struggling to fly.

Ryan tried to speak but found his mouth full of something. He attempted to reach for his lips but his arms wouldn't move.

Where am I? Where's my platoon?

A distant rhythmic beep and hiss slowly came into focus. He forced his eyes wide open and stared at the ceiling vent above. He craned his neck slowly and took in his surroundings. Machines circled his hospital bed—wilted flowers in a vase on a table.

How long have I been here?

His right leg was elevated by pulleys, his left arm cinched tight against his waist. Ryan lay that way for minutes or hours—he couldn't tell.

A face above him—a woman. She adjusted something.

Look at me!

He attempted to speak, but all that came out was the faint rasp of his vocal chords.

She glanced down. Dark hair framed a surprised expression that broke into a smile. "Well, hello there, Sergeant Turner. Good to see you with us."

Ryan tried to speak or move his hands. Nothing.

"I'm your nurse, Sherry. I expect you've got some catching up to do." Her voice had a slight southern accent—soft and warm, like fresh baked bread.

Ryan wrinkled his forehead with desperate questions.

Sherry reached up and stroked his forehead with a caring hand.

Ryan began to cry.

"Everything's going to be fine." She patted his arm with her other hand. "You're at the Army's Landstuhl Regional Medical Center, we call it LRMC—in Germany. You've been with us about three weeks now. Didn't know when you'd wake up."

She grabbed a tissue and wiped his tears like his mother did when Ryan was a small boy.

Mom. Dad.

Memories of them laying in their blood on the kitchen floor jolted him. The vision of Russell Stephens' dark face and wild hair—the man who murdered them—flooded his mind.

"You can't move your arms because of restraints—in case you woke up and tried to get out of bed. I'll get Doctor Carruthers and we'll see what we can do about getting you off the ventilator."

***

Two days later, after reviewing a series of x-rays of his right leg and left shoulder, Ryan bobbed his head in understanding.

"Could have been worse," Doctor Carruthers said, his hands pointing to spots on the tablet screen he held. "Notice the rod and screws we put in your femur?"

"Yes," Ryan said. He looked to Sherry, who nodded.

The doctor continued, "Your leg was shattered to the point we thought we'd lose it or you'd get sepsis. You had a crack team of orthopedic surgeons piecing you back together—nicknamed you Humpty Dumpty. With some serious PT, the most you should have is a slight limp. Nothing to keep the girls away." He grinned, his 40-something face speaking the truth.

"So, what you're telling me is I can still dance?" Ryan returned the grin.

Nurse Sherry patted his arm. "And go bowling too."

Ryan and the doctor chuckled.

"What about my shoulder"? Ryan pressed.

"Shoulder joints are a little more complicated. When you get stateside … by the way, where you from?"

"Michigan. Kalamazoo, Michigan."

"You'll spend some time at Walter Reed first. They have the best orthopedists. Then when you're ready, they'll transfer you to a VA hospital in Saginaw or Ann Arbor. They'll set you up with a rehab schedule and any follow-on work." He patted Ryan on the forearm. "You'll do fine, Sergeant."

"When can I find out what happened to my unit—and rejoin them?"

Sherry cleared her throat and spoke up. "A Marine colonel is scheduled to come by tomorrow to see you. He'll go over everything."

***

"So, that's it, Colonel?" Ryan asked, a slow anger building in him, his hand balled into a fist.

"Your injuries were so extensive, they preclude you from future combat. You could put in for a desk job…" Colonel Ambrose rose from the chair he'd sat in for the half-an-hour debriefing Ryan. "Things'll make a lot more sense when you get stateside, Sergeant Turner. Follow the plan they put in front of you for rehab—for your physical well-being and as well as counseling. You went through a lot. Maybe when all this settles, you can take advantage of the GI Bill and go back to school." He took hold of Ryan's right hand and shook it.

Ryan wouldn't let go of the colonel's hand. "So, only five Marines besides me made it? Where are they?"

"Most are stateside. One, I believe, is still…" his voice faded and he turned his head slightly like he was sorry he mentioned it.

Ryan wouldn't let go of his hand, his connection to the truth. "Who?"

"You don't want to see him—not in his condition."

"Who is it?"

"Nuñez." The colonel clenched his teeth like he'd been gut punched.

Ryan let go of the colonel's hand. "What's wrong with him?"

The colonel let out a sigh, as if he told this same kind of story a thousand times. "He's on life support, no brain activity. His next of kin are here deciding what to do."

Those aching words hung in the air.

"I want to see him."

***

The orderly raised Ryan's wheelchair so he could see Nuñez. Ryan gulped. Nuñez stared ahead with vacant eyes, a ventilator, feeding tubes, and intravenous lines keeping him alive. A monitor displayed a steady heartbeat. The EEG noted the flat line of his brain activity.

"Can I be alone with him for a few minutes?" Ryan asked the orderly.

"Just let me know when you're finished," the orderly said walking out the door.

Ryan leaned in to Nuñez and whispered, "They say you can't hear anything. Well, you never did listen too good." He grinned and took hold of Nuñez' hand, avoiding the tubes sticking out of it. He sat that way for a few minutes, then patted Nuñez' hand, and let out a soft "oorah."

Ryan wiped a tear from his face, straightened up, and called out, "I'm ready."

***

After getting cleared to leave Germany and transported to Maryland, it was a week before Ryan was situated in a shared room at Walter Reed National Military Medical Center. Again, his leg was elevated by a series of pulleys and his right arm strapped against his belly.

He looked out the window at the fountain, water flowing over from one level to another, cascading in sheets—peaceful—nothing like he felt. Anxious wasn't quite the right word. Nervous was closer—about the endless rehab ahead of him.

A large black bird landed on his windowsill, staring at Ryan, tilting its head from side to side as if he wanted to ask a question.

Ryan closed his eyes and dozed off.

He woke when a voice from the bed next to him called out, "Goddammit!"

Ryan couldn't see the soldier due to the heavy blue curtain separating them.

"Where's the fucking nurse?" the soldier yelled.

"Hey," Ryan said. "Push the fucking red button."

"My goddamn fucking bag is leaking."

Ryan pushed his button and half a minute later a nurse entered the room. He thumbed toward the curtain and shrugged his shoulder. Ryan listened in as the nurse cleaned up the mess. From what he could make out, his roommate was Lieutenant Thomas from Philadelphia and his intestines were scrambled due to shrapnel from an IED.

The nurse, a blonde in her mid-thirties, checked on Ryan before she left. "Need anything, Sergeant?"

"Prime rib—medium rare, if you got it." He grinned. "What's your name?"

"Donna." She repositioned him, fluffed his pillows, and checked his fluid levels. She paused before heading for the door. "Any sides with that?"

***

The months dragged by with operations and physical therapy. They removed the rod and screws from Ryan's leg. He had two operations on his shoulder, the last one including a new joint. When he was cleared for PT, Ryan did exactly as the doctors instructed, plus a little more. Tearing through the tight scar tissue that built up was almost as bad as when the bullets struck—only it lasted longer. That pain was nothing compared to the grief he felt for the 37 Marines who lost their lives to the Taliban with him as their platoon leader.

Aunt Morgan called every week and was prepared to come visit Ryan, but he insisted she wait until he came home to Kalamazoo. One thing she did mention caught his attention.

"Looks like the trial of that Stephens man is finally going to happen," she said.

"It's been two years. Why isn't it over?"

"The papers say he's changed lawyers several times." She paused. "And there's some technicalities they're sorting out."

Ryan sat up in his bed. "Like what?"

"Something about the way they handled the arrest and some of the DNA tests. I don't know much about that."

The phone went silent, Ryan at a loss as to what to say. He stared at the muted TV, Alex Trebek reading from the category of State Capitals about Maine.

What is Augusta?

"Yeah. Well, thanks for calling, Aunt Morgan. Talk to you soon."

"I love you, Ryan."

"Okay."

***

After a few outbursts, one where he threw his tray filled with food across the chow hall, he was prompted to go to counseling.

Dr. Marston, a 50-something psychologist and Major in the Army, started their first session with getting-to-know-you questions. "How they treating you here?" "Where you from, Sergeant?" "Mind if I call you Ryan?" "Play sports at all when you were in school?" "How did you feel when the police caught your parents' killer?"

It took a while before Ryan gave the answers the major wanted—ones that wouldn't prompt more questions. After their third session, he asked about Ryan's time in the service, starting with boot camp, then focusing on Ryan's first tour as a sniper. "Twenty-three kills. How did that make you feel?"

Good.

"Just doing my job, Sir," he answered.

During their sixth session, Major Marston got into Ryan's second tour of duty at FOB Delaram, *Home of the Darkside.* When the major reached the morning of Ryan's departure on his last mission, Ryan was hit by a massive migraine.

"You alright, Sergeant?"

Ryan reeled, nausea throttling his body. He grabbed the major's trash can and wretched, convulsions of vomit wracking him for a few minutes.

"Migraine, Doc," he gasped. Ryan wiped his mouth with the back of his hand, stood, and snatched his cane. "Gotta go." He hobbled out of the Major's office.

That's the last time I talk to anyone about that.

13

KENNEDY

Easton's second year was punctuated by more of Linda injecting herself into his life—insisting he accompany her, and Kennedy as well, to the opera, cruise the Mediterranean, and winter vacation in Switzerland. "You've got to expose him at an early age to culture and travel. Look how well-adjusted Logan was?"

Well-adjusted? He was a monster.

Linda brushed Easton's long blond hair away from his eyes. "Easton, when is your mommy going to cut your hair? You're starting to look like one of those hippies."

"I was going to let it grow a little bit longer. His first haircut will be special," Kennedy said and swept Easton's hair back and held it in place with a scrunchie.

Linda shook her head in disappointment. "With his long hair, sometimes people think he's a girl. Is that what you want?"

"Kids at his age don't care about hair or fashion. Only their parents and grandparents do."

Linda gave off a disapproving shake of her head. "Well, you let me know when he's ready for his first haircut. I'll take him to Adolfo. He'll make him look like a handsome young man should."

***

"It's never too young to start him in preschool—now that he's potty trained and walking," Linda said while bouncing Easton on her knee. He burped up a little mess and she handed him back to Kennedy as if he was contagious.

Kennedy cleaned his chin with a baby wipe, an ever-present remedy. "He's only sixteen months old, Linda. Let's give him some time to improve his language skills so he can communicate with the teachers and other kids."

Linda shook her head. "I don't know. I heard that the Benneton's child, who's Easton's age, well, he's been put into an advanced learning curriculum at a prestigious preschool. I checked. They allow only the best. And just look at him. Aren't you just the smartest little boy in the world? Just like your daddy." Linda tried to tickle Easton but he wriggled out of Kennedy's grasp and ran to play with a toy train.

Linda looked on adoringly and sighed. "I see more and more of Logan in him every day. Don't you?"

He's not Logan's child!

She wanted to scream the words at Linda but instead smiled and nodded.

"This isn't right." Linda's face crinkled as she stood to rearrange flowers in a vase on the coffee table.

***

Kennedy put together a small picnic to celebrate Easton's second birthday and her guest list didn't include Linda. Eight of Easton's friends and their mothers, from play dates at the park, came with simple gifts and big smiles. There were balloons, chocolate cake, and strawberry ice cream—everything a group of two-year-olds could want. Kennedy planned it to take place two days before Linda's birthday party for Easton.

Linda went all out, besting his first birthday party in every way, the theme changing from the big top to a salute to the golden age of music and movies. To impress her friends, she flew in Tony Bennett and his orchestra. When he sang "Happy Birthday" to Easton, tears streamed down her face.

***

A month later, on the Saturday evening of Linda's Heart Association Gala, Kennedy stood by the front door of her condo for the last time. She glanced in the hallway mirror. Her long black hair was braided and stuffed under a baseball cap.

I look 18, not 25.

She held Easton's hand and looked down at him. Beside her were two suitcases packed with their lives. They each wore a backpack, his stuffed with a shark from the Sea World gift shop, his favorite Tonka truck, and snacks for the long trip ahead.

She planned for this moment since the day Easton was born. Not a trace. No car. No phone. No email or Facebook anymore. She left them all behind, never to be used again. She had weaned herself from her friends and slowly cut all social ties. Their clothes were from Goodwill but didn't look too poor. That's also where she got their suitcases.

Kennedy glanced at the envelope on the coffee table. She chose the words carefully on the enclosed letter, not wishing to completely burn the bridge she was about to cross.

Linda –

Easton and I are going away. It's nothing you've done. We want to create a life for ourselves, without Logan's memory and money hanging over us. You have been a wonderful grandmother, giving so much of yourself.

We'll be in touch once we get settled and we're ready. Please don't come looking for us—it'll only make matters worse. This is my decision alone, and I believe it's best for Easton.

I hope your gala went well tonight.

Kennedy and Easton

Cash. Everything had to be paid in cash. Kennedy had $10,000 in small bills. She shredded her credit and debit cards and purchased fake IDs for her and Easton—they were now Kay and David Goodtree. She carried a backpack stuffed with five hundred $2,000 cashier's checks from banks she knew Linda would never think of. A million dollars to help start a new life. A burner phone, with the GPS deactivated, was her only connection to the electronic world.

They took a taxi to Lindbergh Field, hopped in another to Horton Plaza's Grand Hotel, and took another to the Greyhound Bus terminal. Kennedy was glad she brought lots of baby wipes, Easton exploring everything like a two-year-old can.

Kennedy took Easton's hand, wandered over to the ticket counter, and got in line. "Try not to touch anything, okay?" Kennedy warned, hugging Easton so his hands couldn't reach anything.

"Ah-chee, where we going?" Easton looked up to her.

"On an adventure. We'll see mountains and rivers and—"

"Next!" a voice called out from the ticket counter.

Kennedy shuffled the two suitcases up to the window where a balding man with kind eyes looked them over.

He looked down at Easton. "Where might you be going?"

"On a 'venture," Easton said with a grin.

The man smiled and looked to Kennedy. "And where would *venture* be?"

Kennedy desperately tried not to look desperate but to look like she belonged. "Two tickets to San Francisco, please. One adult, one child."

***

Their bus showed up half an hour later at nine o'clock. Kennedy watched their suitcases stowed beneath the bus in the cargo hold. They boarded and got seats in the back, Easton by the window. She placed their backpacks on the floor under their seats.

After an hour, Easton leaned against his mother's chest and fell asleep—the rhythm and warmth of his breath reminding her of the day he was born—the happiest day of her life.

She brushed strands of blond hair off his forehead and watched him slowly smack his lips, ending with a smile.

Kennedy whispered in his ear, "We're going home."

***

Kennedy woke to a pair of dark eyes peering at her through the space between the two blue seats in front of her. She squinted at the person then looked at her watch—after one o'clock.

A woman's head appeared above the seat, a mop of curly brown hair framing a chubby face and dark skin. "Hi," she said plopping her arms on the top of the seat and resting her chin on them.

"Trouble sleeping?" Kennedy asked.

"Yeah. Hey, where's your husband?" the woman asked.

"Excuse me?" Kennedy asked.

"Sorry, I noticed the rock on your finger—and the cute little boy is all."

Kennedy looked at her left hand.

Crap. I was supposed to leave that behind.

"He's not with me. My husband, that is."

"I can see that." The woman squinted her eyes. "I know a runner when I see one," the woman smirked.

"What?" Kennedy tried to act confused.

How do you know?

"You're leaving your husband. Why else would you be on a bus heading to San Francisco?"

"No, that's not the case." Kennedy took a deep breath. "My husband died three years ago."

"Oh." The woman stuck out her hand. "By the by, I'm Nicole."

Kennedy shook it. "I'm Heather."

"Where's your final destination, Heather?" Nicole asked wide-eyed.

"Going home."

Easton tossed and turned.

Kennedy looked down at him. "We really need to get our sleep. Nice meeting you, Nicole."

Nicole stared at her for a few moments, then her face lit up. "Oh, sorry. I can get gabbing. Good night. Oh, I mean good morning."

Kennedy gave a tired smile. "Good morning to you too, Nicole."

***

Someone shook Kennedy's shoulder.

"Ma'am, we're in San Francisco. Time to get off," a voice said.

Kennedy rubbed her eyes awake, realized the bus was empty, and reached over for Easton—nothing. Her eyes widened. "Where's my son?"

"Your son?" asked the overweight bus driver.

She jumped up. "Easton! Easton!" She pushed past the bus driver and ran toward the front.

"He just went outside with your friend."

Kennedy wheeled around. "My friend?"

The bus driver pointed out the window. "Yeah, she's there with your bags."

Kennedy rushed out the door and found Easton holding Nicole's hand. Nicole wore her backpack.

What the hell are you doing?

It was everything she could do to keep from making a scene.

"I see you met Nicole." Kennedy crouched down to look Easton over and took his hand from Nicole.

"He's fine." Nicole smiled and adjusted Kennedy's backpack. "I guess I'll be going."

121

Kennedy put her hand on Nicole's shoulder, grabbing hold of the backpack strap. "I don't think so. You've got my backpack."

"No, this isn't yours. Yours is on the bus. I have one just like it." Nicole leaned in to whisper, "I bet yours is worth lots of money."

Crap. What do you want?

Out of the corner of her eye, Kennedy noticed the bus driver pause outside the bus and watch them. She turned with a slight smile and nodded to him then looked back at Nicole. Keeping her voice low, Kennedy let out a sigh. "What do you want?"

"A finder's fee. I took care of your boy while you were sleeping and guarded your backpack. What do you think is fair?"

Nothing, you bitch.

Kennedy assessed Nicole, really taking her in. JC Penney clothes, maybe Target, store bought jewelry, no wedding ring.

My ring.

"Tell you what—how about my ring? You said you liked it." Kennedy held it up to Nicole's face. "Five carats—it's worth fifty thousand. Any jeweler will give you at least twenty-five."

"I like your backpack better." Nicole picked up her suitcase and turned to leave.

"No! I mean, no." Kennedy reached out and touched her arm. "What do you want?"

"To win the lottery—not all—maybe what a scratcher would pay. It'd go a long way to getting Daryl back." She sniffed and wiped her nose with the back of her hand.

"That sounds like ten thousand to me," Kennedy said almost in a question.

"I was thinking more like fifty," Nicole said looking around to see if anyone watched.

"How about we split the difference at thirty?"

"Forty and you got a deal."

Forty to be done with you?

"Okay. I'll give you twenty cashier's checks."

Nicole crinkled her forehead and took a cautious step back.

"Nicole, they're just like cash. That's twenty checks—at two thousand each—that's forty thousand dollars. Would Daryl like that?"

"Would I have to pay taxes?"

"No."

Nicole scratched her hair and inspected something she picked out of it.

Easton tugged on Kennedy's hand and she looked down. "Ah-chee, juicy juice?"

"In a minute, sweetheart." Kennedy turned to Nicole. "Well?"

"I kinda like the ring too." Nicole looked at Kennedy with hopeful eyes.

Kennedy put her wedding finger in her mouth and pulled it off—the ring now resting on the tip of her tongue.

Nicole smiled. "Okay. Let's go to the coffee shop. I'll even buy you breakfast."

***

For half an hour, Kennedy listened to Nicole go on about Daryl and their big plans. It seemed nothing would stop her.

Kennedy slid an envelope across the table to Nicole and stood, grabbing her backpack and ushering Easton out of the booth. "We've got to get going."

Nicole pouted. "Really? We're just getting to know each other."

"Yes, really." Kennedy hefted the backpack and grabbed Easton's hand. "Good luck with your life."

A slight nod from Nicole and Kennedy and Easton left the coffee shop—not daring to look back.

They took a taxi to the train station. Riding in a sleeper car, they'd be in Billings, Montana, in thirty-seven hours fifty-eight minutes. From there, it was another hour by bus to the comforting arms of Miss Betty Old Horn on the Crow Reservation.

The miles meant nothing to Kennedy, home everything.

They watched a new world pass outside the window of their sleeper car, Easton on Kennedy's lap busy pointing and asking, "Ah-chee, what's that?" again and again.

"That's our future and next adventure, Easton."

He looked up at her and smiled. "Venture."

14

RYAN

Ryan stepped off the plane and it hit him—Kalamazoo—about as middle America as it could be. There was a smell to it—old, tired, full of memories. As he walked through the airport, he noticed things had changed. People seemed familiar but different. Was it their smiles? Something in the way they moved? It hit him.

You have purpose.

Ryan didn't need his cane anymore to walk but used it to have something to hold onto. Aunt Morgan was there to greet him at baggage claim. She wore a blue dress Ryan hadn't seen her in before, her gray hair put up nice. She paused a moment when she saw him, confusion on her face. That's when he realized how different he must look and that she hadn't seen him in 18 months. He was twenty-five pounds lighter, blond hair grown out, and had a scruffy beard. She hugged him hard anyway.

The five-mile drive home felt longer with Aunt Morgan's non-stop chatter, bringing Ryan up to speed on everything Kalamazoo—everything except Russell Stephens.

Ryan limped into his bedroom and took it in. It was just the way he left it—except Aunt Morgan put up new white lacy curtains, got a new lamp, and set out a vase with fresh flowers. "Nice. Really nice," he said and felt it.

"Oh, it's nothing," Aunt Morgan gushed and gave Ryan another hug—the fifth since he saw her. "You get settled and come to the kitchen when you're ready. I've made you a special dinner." She beamed, patted him on the arm, and moved down the hall humming.

He hobbled to the closet and opened it. The gray and green jacket of the East Michigan Eagles caught his eye. *One week.* That's all the time he spent in college. *That was three years ago. I wonder if...* he let his thoughts drift as he stepped over to the window and glanced out.

Birds chirped. Kids played on the sidewalk. Neighbors mowed grass. Cars drove by slowly, going somewhere, a destination ahead of them.

No one murdered your parents.

The thought startled him and Ryan grew rigid. A few moments later, he relaxed enough to let the idea take hold. Like a weed in the crack of a sidewalk determined to grow—all it needed was a little light, water, and soil to take root.

Kalamazoo was just the place for that.

Russell Stephens, you're my destination.

***

Ryan Turner received 100% disability from the Marines, a pension of sorts for the rest of his life—$2,362 a month. He came away with a right leg one inch shorter, an artificial left shoulder that would never get arthritis, a Purple Heart, an honorable discharge—and dark memories. If he chose, he could live the rest of his life with Aunt Morgan until she died, inherit her home, and do nothing. Other wounded warriors who couldn't work, or lost the initiative, did the same. Some took to alcohol, drugs, or worse—homelessness a common aftermath—suicide another path. He heard all the stories as part of his counseling. He wasn't interested in that kind of life.

"The VA will be there for you," he must have heard fifty times.

The Marines who died under his command—their next of kin received a lump sum of $100,000. In a way, those Marines were lucky—it was over for them.

He couldn't bury those memories but there was one memory Ryan was determined to erase.

***

Ryan accumulated nine months' pay during his hospitalization and recovery—over $30,000. He used $10,000 for a down payment on a brand new 2007 maroon Ford F-150 Barricade with a bull bar—monthly payments of only $450. With Ryan's limp and his VA card, the dealer threw in a bed liner, mud flaps, and top-of-the line CD player and speakers.

The remaining money, well, he had plans for that.

Ryan's father bought him his first small game hunting rifle, a Remington .22, when he was eight years old. On Target Guns & Gunsmithing, located in the heart of Kalamazoo, became their go-to store for anything hunting related.

Freddie, the owner's son, recognized Ryan as soon as he hobbled in the door.

"Hey, Ryan," he said as he lugged his 300 pounds and Grizzly Adams beard over to Ryan.

They spent a few minutes catching up, then Freddie asked, "Whatcha looking for?"

"Something custom, like the rifle I fired in the Marines." Ryan looked Freddie in the eyes. "Schmidt and Bender PM II 3–12×50 scope or better. Maybe a longer custom barrel."

"Sniper type. What kind of game you lookin' to take down at a thousand yards?"

"Don't know if I'll go back to hunting." Ryan set his cane on the counter. "Thinking of getting into competitive shooting."

Freddie grinned and stroked his beard. He raised an eyebrow. "Hey, well, if it's for competition, and I assume open class, I gotta M40A5 we can customize."

"That's what I want."

"Might take a few months to get it right—and could run up to seven or eight grand with the case and ammo."

"Whatever it takes."

***

Ryan spent the next few months getting used to Aunt Morgan's fussing, meals, and schedule. Three days a week he drove the 30 miles each way to the VA Medical Center in Battle Creek. There he continued his physical therapy for both his shoulder and leg. They tried to get him in for group counseling but he always found an excuse not to go.

Sixteen and a half pounds—that's all he needed to be able to handle. Strong steady arms and hands that may have to wait hours. He worked hard to build up his upper body and strengthen his legs. Lots of curls, squats, presses, and core building. He was fitted for a custom one-inch lift for his right shoe—making it easier on his hips and back—improving his stride, nearly taking away his limp.

His trainer at the VA, tried to get Ryan to pace himself. "Slow down, Turner, or you're gonna break something."

"Taking it to the breaking point, no more," Ryan said between sets, grunting as he pushed himself the last few reps of chest presses of 200 pounds, his left shoulder muscles feeling the strain.

***

Ryan joined the Kalamazoo Rod & Gun Club, a hundred acres dedicated to sportsmen—all kinds of ranges for firing weapons. Eight to nine-thirty a.m. was his scheduled time every day. Weeks before his rifle was ready, he came out to measure the density altitude and charted the readings in his log book. He got to meet some of the regulars too.

Ryan had seen Donny, an 81-year-old veteran, puttering around the club and asked him about being his spotter. "There's a hundred bucks in it for you, Donny."

Donny was a weathered survivor of the Korean and Vietnam Wars. He mumbled to himself most the time and always wore a ball cap. He could, however, pick up the vapor trail off a round better than anyone else. "Just tell me when. I'm always here," he mumbled.

***

Ryan set up his bipod and sand bag for prone target practice, put on glasses, and inserted his ear plugs.

"Where you want me?" Donny asked, holding the powerful spotter's scope.

Ryan dropped to his knees. "Where you usually set up?"

"Right behind you is best." Donny yanked a soiled blue rag out of a rear pocket and coughed something into it.

A bird cawed overhead. Ryan and Donny looked up. Circling directly above them was a large crow. A shudder ran through Ryan—a large black bird—a snowy sand wash on the other side of the world—too cold to smell death.

Donny shielded his eyes against the bright sky. "Damn, never seen anything like that. Birds stay clear of the range."

Ryan shook his head clear. He lay down in the prone position, the rifle steady on the bipod. He slid out the bolt of his single-shot sniper rifle and sighted through the bore to an 8x10 target a hundred yards away. He placed the first .308 cartridge, a 175-grain CR Match Grain, into the chamber. He inserted the bolt and closed it.

Ryan lifted his rifle off the sandbag, his fingers tingling just like they did in Afghanistan.

No need to adjust for wind speed or direction at a hundred yards. No need to adjust for any drop. Just breath and heartbeat.

Ryan sighted, waited between heartbeats, and fired, the recoil surging through his cheek and right shoulder deliciously. He shot a grouping of three, Donny providing call outs for adjustments after each shot. Ryan took a single shot to set his initial zero and logged it in his ledger.

Two hundred yards, no bore sighting this time. Three shot grouping. Triangulated and adjusted with Donny's call outs. Single shot. Dead center. Logged it.

"I know it's only two hundred yards, but hole-ee shit," Donny said as took his eyes off the spotter's scope, an unlit cigarette dangling from his cracked brown lips. "Damn, fine setup, Ryan. They teach you that in the corps?"

Ryan ignored his question and stood. "Wanna help me with something?"

"Sure," Donny said and shrugged.

Ryan opened a box and took out a square orange instrument with a series of buttons and a flat panel display, no bigger than a clipboard.

"What's that?" Donny asked, cautiously squinting at the contraption like it came off a UFO.

"It's a ballistic velocity doppler radar chronograph," Ryan said as he mounted it on a tripod low to the ground.

Donny lifted his worn Earl Scheib ballcap and scratched his thin gray hair. "Damn if I know what you're talking about."

"It measures muzzle velocity. Higher loads mean less drop over distance. This gives me a baseline for 175 loads. All scientific."

Donny gave Ryan a toothy grin. "Okay, Mr. Scientist, what next?"

"We'll lock it into the 200-yard target and shoot a few rounds," Ryan answered while he sighted the instrument. He pressed a few buttons on the back of the screen.

Satisfied, he lowered himself to the prone shooting position, loaded a cartridge, and fired. He did this three times, each time logging the numbers Donny called out. Ryan took the device off the tripod and put it back in the box.

"That's it?" Donny asked.

"That's it. Now, I need you to spot me every hundred yards. Let's do some from a standing position too." It was two years since Ryan put a bullet through a raghead. Ryan lifted his rifle off the bipod, hefting the 16-½ pounds. It felt light. "And let's use silhouettes."

***

Ryan worked up a good sweat by the time they finished an hour later. His notations filled a few pages in his log book. Like he learned in Marine sniper school in Hawaii—shoot and record. He had his initial DOPE—Data of Previous Engagement.

I need a few more.

He slipped Donny a hundred-dollar bill.

"You didn't have ta," Donny said, but gladly stuffed the money in a front pocket, then lit his cigarette, a satisfying grin spreading across his wrinkled face as he took a slow drag.

"Same time tomorrow?" Ryan asked.

"Sure," Donny answered, smoke seeping out of his nose and mouth.

***

To keep Ryan from getting upset, Aunt Morgan kept anything Russell Stephens-related from him, canceling the morning newspaper and stopping cable TV. Ryan knew what she was doing so he picked up the local paper every day on his way to the range and read it during his stationary bike time at the VA. Friday morning, four days from then, Russell Stephens was scheduled in court, being bused over from the county jail to arrive for a nine o'clock hearing.

Ryan would be in position by eight.

He scouted places in the area and found a three-story office building, a perfect spot on the roof. No security cameras. Easy building access. That's where he took his density altitude readings—the data that could change the trajectory of his 175-grain round. He used a digital range finder—762 yards away from the courthouse steps.

You'll never hear the shot. You'll be dead before the sound arrives.

They wouldn't know where it came from. Even if they did somehow figure it out, he didn't care. He'd spend the rest of his life in prison, a small price for what Russell Stephens did to his parents.

***

Six-thirty, Friday morning.

As usual, Ryan found Aunt Morgan in the kitchen. She wore a faded green apron over a house dress and turned when he walked in, a puzzled expression on her face. "Where you going all dressed up?" She placed two slices of French toast on a plate and set it on the kitchen table.

Ryan sat down and adjusted his tie, the first time he wore one since his parents' funeral.

That was three years ago.

"Got a job interview," he answered, pouring Aunt Jemimah syrup on the warm egg-soaked raisin bread. "I love the extra nutmeg and cinnamon you put in it." Ryan smiled at her and dug into his plate.

Yeah, I got a job interview.

15

RYAN

It was simple math. Ryan added it up—762 yards, 16½ pounds, one dead murderer. Three years ago, Russell Stephens took Ryan Turner's life and turned it inside out, murdering his parents and setting his tarot cards on fire. Now it was Ryan's time to take control of his fate.

He parked behind the three-story office building, careful no cameras could spot his coming or going. He took off his tie and put on a pair of baggy soiled coveralls with an Amstead H/VAC patch above his right pocket, the name Darryl on the left. Ryan wore gloves and tucked his blond hair beneath a beanie cap, not uncommon for a chilly Kalamazoo morning—but they added an extra layer of disguise.

Ryan got out of his pickup, reached into the cargo bed, and lugged a large tool box through a side door that automatically unlocked at 7 am—it was 7:12. He wound his way up two flights of stairs to the service entrance to the roof. He paused at the bottom of the ladder and listened. They city was just waking up—a low hum of muffled activity outside. Nothing in the building. He took a pair of bolt cutters out of his toolbox, climbed the ladder, and severed the MasterLock's shackle with a snap.

He scrambled down to retrieve his toolbox and made his way back up the ladder, through the hatch, and up onto the roof. A light breeze, the kind that wouldn't alter the flight of a high-velocity round, greeted him. He looked around. There was only one taller building with windows that had a view of the roof, and it was three blocks away. From where he would set up, no one could see what he was up to.

He lugged his tool box to the northeast corner of the building and set it down behind the three-foot high facade, the large H/VAC system nearby providing complete cover. He assembled his rifle in under two minutes and set the log book next to it. Ryan was surprised at how calm he felt—like the Marines taught him—to keep his heart beat low and breathing exercises to clear his head. He was on the battlefield now. In position.

He looked at his watch—7:31. A burp teased out of his stomach into his mouth. Aunt Morgan's French toast and coffee—a reminder to him of how small his life had become and it didn't taste good.

Aunt Morgan.

Aunt Morgan, with her ever-cheerful smile and kind ways.

If I get caught, I hope you understand.

He lay down in position, flipped the cap off his scope, and scanned the courthouse—shadows around it slowly disappearing as the sun rose. An Umi poem came to mind from his lit class during the one week he attended Eastern Michigan University. He liked it at the time but didn't know why.

What was it? Something about shadows. Ah, yes.

"Of ones heart with shadows lurking to take over spite is made precious to be felt exciting while it is in fact trecious, but a sleeping terror awakens at times..."

Something like that.

He smiled at the fact he remembered it at all.

A bird "cawed" overhead and Ryan craned his neck to look up—puzzled—a crow.

Are you the same bird from the range?

He watched it circle overhead, let out a few more caws, and make its way to a large oak by the courthouse and rest on a branch near the top facing Ryan.

What are you up to?

Ryan shook his head clear and went over the DOPE details again in his log book. Same temperature today—it was supposed to be 46 degrees at 8:45. The faded white bus would pull up with the prisoners at that time, marshals and sheriff's deputies escorting them up the steps. He stopped by the courthouse a dozen times after the range to watch their drill.

Russell Stephens would be in a blue jumpsuit—most likely the only one on the chain, his wrists cuffed to a waist chain linked to ankle chains. One deputy on each side of him, one hand on the waist chain, another holding an elbow. Ryan calculated he had between four and five seconds to take his shot—in the middle of his back, below his shoulder blades—through his heart.

Today they were supposed to start the trail—*after three fucking years*. Once it was over, supposedly within a week, Ryan would be asked to come to the sentencing as the lone family member to tell the court to have no mercy. Russell couldn't get the death penalty, life in prison the best they could do under Michigan law. Ryan would change that today.

He looked at his watch—8:04—then back to the scope. The doors of the courthouse were open now. Lawyers, followed by assistants lugging mounds of paper and exhibits, plodded up the steps of justice—*ha*—justice? For three years, Russell Stephen's public defenders trudged him through the *justice* system with motions and delays, countless assessments for his ability to comprehend the charges against him—to the point where nothing moved. Like a plugged toilet full of shit.

Today I'll unclog it.

Ryan got up and grabbed a thermos out of his tool box, opened it, took a long swig of Gatorade, sat with his back against the wall, and closed his eyes. Images of fishing and hunting with his father, fireflies on the lake during warm summers, mom always cooking up something delicious for 'her boys.' The memories were warm, like a soft blanket. He lingered there for a few minutes until a siren startled Ryan out of his thoughts. It was close by.

He looked at his watch—8:17—and peeked over the edge. A fire truck headed down the street to an accident that clogged an intersection four blocks away. He dropped down and viewed the action through his scope. Two dented vehicles. One injury—minor. Six cops on the scene, two handling traffic. One ambulance with two EMTs. Four firemen dressed to tackle any emergency. Most stood around and chatted with their counterparts. On a day like today, in a town the size of Kalamazoo, with its 72,000 residents, this was an exciting as it got for a Friday morning.

Someone from the diner on a corner brought out coffee and muffins for the emergency personnel. The entire scene unfolded in slow motion, like watching grass grow.

I wonder where you'll be going at 8:50?

Ryan glanced at his watch—8:33.

Time to go to work.

***

Ryan already had a 175-grain .308 cartridge in the chamber, the scope sighted on the middle of the steps. A five-and-a-half-inch drop over the 762 yards. There was no cross wind to worry about. He clicked the safety off. The bus pulled up at 8:46.

Prisoners began to unload—but not Russell yet. He felt his heart race and worked to calm it. "Come on down, get below sixty," he mumbled.

The bus was nearly empty and he wondered if the court changed its mind about Russell Stephens. He worked to calm his anxious mind. There was a small commotion on the other side of the bus—it looked like with the last prisoner—Russell! Ryan could tell by his dark stringy hair. They were trying to move him and he wasn't cooperating.

The deputies dragged him toward the steps, Ryan getting a quick peek at him through the bus windows. He was almost clear now—his head about to appear over the roof of the bus. Ryan placed his finger on the trigger, calmed his breath, felt his heart beat, and waited.

A loud "caw" nearly broke his concentration. The wind stirred around him, compressing in billowing gusts. Another "CAW" that hurt his ears.

Russell's head came into view through the scope.

"Caw."

Wings beat about Ryan but he couldn't stop.

The deputies moved Russell one step up toward the halls of justice.

"CAW!"

His finger began to squeeze.

Russell's upper body came into view, filling Ryan's scope.

Blackness—beating wings—"CAW!"

Ryan took his finger off the trigger and jerked his head up. The crow rested on the barrel of the rifle in front of the scope. It looked unwaveringly at Ryan, a knowing look in its eyes.

Ryan opened his mouth to yell at the bird but, at the moment, the panic and anger of losing his chance at justice drained from him. He turned and retched his breakfast onto the roof. After he finished convulsing, Ryan wiped his mouth against his sleeve, and looked at the crow. It simply stared back at him, hanging on his barrel, cocking its head from side to side.

"What the fuck do you want?"

The crow simply watched.

Ryan bowed his head and sobbed—deep agonizing tears— for his parents, for his comrades who died under his command in Afghanistan—for his anger and hatred—for everything.

He looked back at the crow, blurry through his tears.

"Well?"

It hopped off the barrel of his sniper rifle onto the roof and stared back. Then it flapped its wings, the torrent air-drying Ryan's tears. Ryan stopped sobbing and stared at the bird.

"What?"

The crow let out a mighty "CAW" and launched into flight, brushing past Ryan's startled face. It rose above him, looking down at Ryan as he looked up at it. It circled overhead once and let out a final "caw," then flew into the morning sun.

Ryan's mouth hung open in awe—emotions flooding him—loss, grief, despair, and hate.

There has to be more to life than this.

He caught a last glimpse of the crow as it veered away from the bright sun, hearing, maybe imagining, it let out one more "caw" and disappeared.

You know something I don't and I'm going to find out what it is.

16

KENNEDY

Kennedy waited two years to make one call on her burner phone, to hear one voice. Before she and Easton boarded the bus in Billings, Montana, she dialed Miss Betty Old Horn, the number scorched into her memory. Instead of Miss Betty answering the call, a voice said, "The number you have reached is no longer in service."

Those words haunted her during the hour bus ride to Crow Nation—wondering, hoping her grandmother would be there for them. The last letter Kennedy wrote begged Miss Betty not to reach out to Kennedy no matter what, to save a place for her and Easton—and to wait.

Kennedy looked down as Easton snuggled into her lap asleep, his long curly blond hair spilling all over her. She caressed his head and stared out the bus window, watching the land rush by, the dark mountains and hills matching the foreboding that came over her.

Where are you, Miss Betty?

***

The bus came to a stop and Kennedy woke Easton with a small shake to his shoulder. She whispered, "We're here, Easton. We're home."

They deboarded, collected their bags, and looked around. Miss Betty Old Horn would feel Kennedy's spirit. She looked at her watch—2:15 pm. She'd wait. Kennedy took their bags and they sat on a park bench across from Crow Tribe Executive Branch. She took off the ball cap she'd been wearing for two days, unbraided her long black hair, and shook it loose in the light breeze.

Kennedy kept Easton busy with snacks and coloring books. When she looked up occasionally, she noticed people staring at them—an Indian woman with a blond curly-haired boy—then she realized how odd they must look. When it reached four o'clock, she lugged their suitcases to the tribal office.

"I'm here to see Miss Betty, Miss Betty Old Horn," she told the clerk.

"Let me see," the short plump woman with tightly braided hair answered. She plodded back to her desk to look at her computer. Kennedy watched the woman navigate the screen and stop, a look of concern on her face. Without glancing up, she went to a row of filing cabinets, opened one, and flipped through the files until she pulled one out. She paused when she opened it to read over the contents. Then she looked at Kennedy with sad eyes.

Coming to the counter, she placed the file down. "Miss Betty passed over a year ago. There were no relatives to contact and she only had one daughter who was listed as passed as well."

"Oh no," Kennedy moaned.

"You knew her?"

"She was my grandmother," Kennedy said through teary eyes.

"What's your name"

"Kennedy You—uh, Kennedy McClennan. I was born here."

"Can I see your tribal card?"

Kennedy's face flushed red. "I don't have one."

"Some other identification then, like a drivers' license or passport with your birthdate and place of birth."

I can't give you my fake IDs.

Kennedy paused and gulped. "I lost all my ID in a fire. Maybe you can look me up?" she asked hopefully.

"Okay." The lady nodded her head and retreated to her computer. "Your date of birth and your mother's name?"

***

Half an hour later, the lady presented Kennedy with her tribal card. "Here you go."

Kennedy stared at the card. "Apsáalooke Crow" was printed on it.

My tribe.

The only daughter of an only daughter, Kennedy was the last of her family line—except for Easton. "Can I get a card for my son as well?"

"Sure." The lady noticed Easton dance around nervously by Kennedy's legs. "I think your boy needs to use the restroom."

Kennedy bent down to ask Easton, "You have to go wee-wee?"

He nodded. "Yes, Ah-chee."

When Kennedy returned with Easton, the lady was still at the counter with Miss Betty's folder open. "She left something for you."

"What?"

"Her home in Lodge Grass and a box of belongings in storage." She reached into the fold of the file. "Here's what you need." She handed Kennedy a set of keys. "Do you know where her home is?"

"It's been fourteen years—I was ten, but I think I can find it."

"Well, you let me know if you have any problems." The lady looked behind Kennedy at a clock on the wall. "We need to close the office now—it's five o'clock."

"Oh, okay." Kennedy bent down and zipped up Easton's jacket, put on his backpack and hers, and lugged their suitcases towards the door.

The lady came around the counter and waited by the door to lock up, watching them struggle with their belongings. "You know, if you want, I can drop you off. I think I know where it is and it's sort of on my way home."

Kennedy sighed. "That'd be so nice."

"I'll meet you out front. Just gimme a minute."

***

The woman behind the counter was Sharon Highwater, she was 37 years old, had three teenage girls, and was still married to her high school sweetheart. Sharon spoke non-stop and filled Kennedy in on the local gossip of the last 14 years, the tribal council rulings, the efforts to try to get the state of Montana to give them a gaming license for a casino.

Twenty minutes later they were at Miss Betty Old Horn's two-bedroom home, south of the Crow Agency in Lodge Grass. It was dark, the front yard overgrown with weeds. Sharon turned into the driveway and kept her headlights on. She pulled out a flashlight from under her seat. "Wait here. I'll be right back."

Kennedy watched Sharon walk up to a broken window and shine her flashlight inside. She stepped back quickly, and scurried back to the car. She got in, locked the doors, and tried to catch her breath.

"What is it?"

"There was a pack of wolves or coyotes eating something," Sharon said shaking. "They looked at me with their shiny black eyes. I had to…" her voice faded.

Kennedy looked at Easton then back to Sharon. "We can't stay here tonight. Can you take us to a motel?"

"Sure."

***

The first thing Kennedy did the next day, after she and Easton had breakfast, was buy a car, a five-year-old 2002 beige Toyota 4Runner with 102,000 miles on it. Like everything else, she paid cash and used her Kay Goodtree ID along with Miss Betty's address for the registration. Next, she drove an hour to Billings to the Rimrock Mall to do some shopping—a car seat, cleaning supplies, and clothes. By the time she finished, the 4Runner was full.

She drove to Miss Betty Old Horn's home with a restless Easton. In the late morning light, she could see what had become of the house—complete neglect. She left Easton in his car seat, afraid he would touch anything inside. "Ah-chee will be right back. Listen to the music." She kept the engine running, cracked the windows, and locked the car.

Kennedy looked in the broken window of the house and listened. Nothing. She unlocked the front door and took out a can of mace. When Kennedy opened the front door, her mouth dropped open. The warm and inviting aromas she remembered, the smiles of abundant love—gone. Stench—she reeled and covered her mouth. Tiptoeing in, she peered around cautiously. It appeared vandals broke in months before, teenagers or homeless people had used it, trash was everywhere, appliances and fixtures ruined, graffiti sprayed on the walls. She crept down the hall to the bedroom she used to sleep in—a lone mattress in the middle of floor showed signs of…

She ran out the front door gagging and got in her car, tears forming in her eyes. She shuddered.

A small voice in the back seat asked, "Ah-chee sad?"

Kennedy wiped her eyes and turned to Easton. "A little. We can't live here now but we'll fix it up, good as new." She patted Easton on the leg and put her car in reverse.

***

It took three months and $60,000, half as much as homes in the area were worth, but when she was finished, Kennedy had her family home back—better than before. New air conditioning and heating, all new kitchen, bath, appliances, and low-maintenance landscaping. One other thing she added as a must-have—a security system. In the back of her mind she knew Linda was relentlessly searching for her and Easton.

She covered her tracks well. The house was still in Miss Betty's name, the car and drivers' license under Kay Goodtree. Only the tribal card listed her as Kennedy McClennan.

How could Linda possibly find me?

***

Kennedy was so busy with renovations she almost forgot about the box Miss Betty left her. A week after they moved into their new home, she went to the storage facility to pick it up. Her name was scrawled on the lamp-size cardboard box. It felt light, like Miss Betty's spirit was inside waiting to give her a message. After putting Easton to bed, she poured herself a glass of wine and opened the box, carefully placing the contents on the living room rug in front of the fireplace.

A large envelope with the birth certificates for Betty, her daughter, and Kennedy. Her cradleboard doll, threadbare and tattered now. She held it close and breathed it in, raw memories of her mother and childhood filling her. She pulled out a prayer wheel used by her grandfather. There were other artifacts—all treasures. The simple wooden kitchen utensils Miss Betty used to stir buffalo stew and Kennedy's other childhood favorites were there. She turned the pages of a small photo album and found pictures of Kennedy's mother and father on their wedding day, when Kennedy was born, and as she grew up.

Kennedy's eyes welled up. She took a sip of wine and leaned back, closing her eyes.

Now, I'm home.

***

Kennedy counted up her money—$870,000 remained. Nicole extorted $40,000 and her ring in San Francisco, $15,000 went for the car, then there were the renovations, and what she spent on travel, food, and hotel stays for three months. There was more than enough for Easton's upbringing, education, and maybe some leftover for his wedding. She got a safety deposit box at the Little Horn State Bank in Hardin where she put the rest of her cashier's checks.

Kennedy joined the First Crow Indians Baptist Church where she met other young mothers with children and began playdates, Easton the only blond-headed boy amongst a sea of black hair. Like all two-and-half year-old boys, he didn't notice.

***

Restless after a few months, Kennedy applied for a job at the Custer Battlefield Trading Post in Crow Agency, twenty minutes north. She started in the gift shop and was trained to work in the coffee shop as well. Her time working in a café in San Diego where she met Logan, came back to her, but not their brief and painful time as husband and wife—it faded, just like the worry that Linda would find them.

Daycare followed, joining the church choir, involvement in tribal activities. Kennedy and Easton settled in.

17

RYAN

Ryan took backroads out to Morrow Lake and parked, tears still threatening to flood his eyes. He parked away from anyone, his head down, and sat for a long spell. He looked up. Far out on the water, a boat bobbed with a lone fisherman—exactly how he felt—alone. Memories of camping, hunting, and fishing with his father filled him. Mother at the camp stove seasoning whatever they brought back—her mighty hunters with their prized kills. There was the time she accidentally dumped a cast iron pan of bluegills into the fire—she was so mad, jumping up and down.

He laughed. The sound of his own voice startled him and he took a deep breath.

Okay, what the fuck do I do now?

His purpose gone—interrupted by a big black bird.

A fucking crow. What do I know about them anyway?

He grabbed his phone and turned it on. A chime indicated voicemail. He had two. The first was Aunt Morgan wondering—no, concerned with how his interview went. The second was from the VA wanting to know if he was going to join their buddy system, pairing two wounded soldiers to provide support for each other. He winced at the idea—one crippled Vet helping another wasn't Ryan's idea of moving on.

The crow landed on the hood of his truck and Ryan flinched in surprise. No caw this time, simply tilting its head from side to side, like he was measuring Ryan.

He stared back. "Not you again."

The bird hopped closer to the windshield and pecked at a windshield wiper.

The crow let out a loud "CAW" and continued to stare at Ryan.

Ryan shrugged his shoulder and held up his hands. "What?"

The crow flapped its wings and launched itself into the air. Ryan found his head on the dashboard craning to spot the bird until it drifted above him out of sight. He started his truck and rolled down his window, peering up into the bright morning sky, finding the black bird. "You want me to follow you?" he yelled.

"CAW," the crow answered and soared west.

Ryan drove after the bird. "This is crazy," he mumbled to himself as he left the lake's entrance and headed east, the crow ahead of him and a few hundred feet above.

He found himself on Route 96 heading towards Kalamazoo. "Where you taking me, bird?" he mumbled.

A faint "caw" answered him.

"Okay."

He was surprised when he turned down the street where Aunt Morgan lived. Ryan smiled. "I got it." He pulled over, looked out his truck window, and waved. "Thanks."

The crow let out a "caw" and turned north. Ryan watched it until became nothing but a small black speck—what his future felt like.

He pulled in the driveway, shut off the engine, and placed a call. "Hey, Aunt Morgan, I hope I'm not bothering you at work. I just got home and heard your message."

"Must have been one interesting interview," she said hopefully.

"Nah. It wasn't a good fit—for either of us." He paused. "I'll find something though. I know it's out there."

"That's a good attitude. See you tonight for supper?"

"Yeah, but I'm taking you out. Have you been to Rustica?"

"Oh, Ryan, that's that fancy European restaurant. I don't know…" her voice trailed off.

"I do. It's a jacket and tie kind of place."

"Ooh, that *is* fancy."

"It'll be fun. See you when you get home, Aunt Morgan."

"That sounds wonderful, Ryan."

***

Ryan took the large toolbox out of his truck and lugged it into the garage. He packed his sniper rifle into its carry case and stared at the fine metal work, its precision, its purpose. He paused a moment then closed the case and snapped it shut.

He drove over to On Target Guns, plopped the case on the counter in front of huge Freddie who was munching on the largest donut Ryan ever saw.

"They glaze a loaf of bread for you?"

"I'm on a diet. I usually order two. What can I do for you, make adjustments?"

"Nah, Freddie, it's not gonna work for me. I want to sell it."

"Man, I don't know about that, Ryan. You can't get anywhere near what you paid for it. Maybe fifty cents on the dollar."

"Do it then," Ryan said, his hands resting on the counter. He felt calm, like purpose was slowly bubbling up somewhere inside him.

"You sure?" Freddie asked.

"Yup," Ryan answered with a conviction that surprised him.

It took half an hour to complete the paperwork and get Ryan a check for $3750. As he shook Freddie's hand, he spotted a thick magazine on the counter, *America's Great Hiking Trails*, and picked it up. He noticed the price—$50.00, and put it back.

"It's yours. Consider it part of the deal," Freddie grinned.

Ryan picked it up and nodded. "Thanks."

***

By the time Aunt Morgan pulled into the driveway, Ryan was bouncing on the balls of his feet like he was on the starting line of a race. As she opened the door, he blurted out, "I know what I'm going to do."

A startled Aunt Morgan grinned. "Well, let me take off my coat and put my purse down, and you can tell me all about it."

"Don't take it off. Remember, I'm taking you out."

She looked him up and down, smiling wide. "So handsome in your suit. Let me get freshened up a bit and—"

"No time," he said, helping her on with her coat and ushering her out the door.

"Oh my."

***

Aunt Morgan stared at Ryan over her desert, her brow wrinkled with concern. "How long did you say it will take again? And how far is it?"

"The Pacific Crest Trail is two thousand six hundred fifty miles long, runs from Mexico to Canada, and takes about five months." Ryan beamed.

"All walking?"

"That's what hiking is." He grinned.

"Why do you want to do that?"

"I've gotta try something, do something." He paused and picked at the corner of his napkin, trying to find the right words. "I don't want this to sound all drama or anything, but I have nothing. No parents. No girlfriend. No job. No friends. Yeah, I get a check every month because I've got a shorter leg and a fake shoulder."

Her eyes watered.

"Oh, I have you—and you've been great. But I—I've got to try something for me, push myself, see what I can do."

"Well, Ryan, I don't know anything about that." She reached over and patted his hand, motherly affection filling her face. "My brother—your father—would be proud of you no matter what you did. Weren't you going to be a forest ranger or something?"

"Yes. And I still might." Ryan glanced down at his dessert plate, half his crème brûlée uneaten. He tapped the crusty top with his spoon then looked up. "It's something I want to do—no, need to do. Part of it is to prove to myself I'm not as hopeless as some of the guys at the VA."

"Maybe you'll be an inspiration for them."

Ryan nodded his head. "Yeah, maybe I will."

***

Ryan was thankful he was in good shape from all his exercise and physical therapy at the VA, the one-inch lift for his shoe helping out, allowing him walk without a limp. He worked out a budget for making the 2,650-mile trek and REI became his go-to place for everything he needed. A two-pound tent cost $400 compared to $140 for a four-pound tent. It was all about weight and durability. He chose lightweight—from his backpack to his boots, clothing, dried food, and water bladders. Ice axe, sleeping bag and pad, flashlight, camp stove and fuel, survival knife, plastic spade—the list seemed endless. It took him two weeks to put it all together.

When Ryan hefted his full 48-pound backpack, he swayed and worked to steady his six-foot-two-inch frame. He remembered his Deuce Gear, the 70-plus-pounds of equipment that he went into combat with in Afghanistan—and the death that accompanied it. He shuddered. That was all behind him now.

He would be thru-hiker, one of 200 or so who attempted to hike the Pacific Crest Trail each year from start to finish with no breaks. Under the urging of his physical therapist, he stopped by the VA the day before he left for the California-Mexico border to visit with some of the guys. He parked his truck outside by the curb. Many of the Vets wheeled out to see Ryan and what he was all about, the questions taking a full hour to answer. Before they went inside, one by one, they shook his hand and said, "Stay in touch," or "See you later," or "Send pictures," and a few with "Oorahs" and bumped fists.

Ryan hadn't thought about people wanting to know what he was up to. On the way back to Aunt Morgan's, he bought a Canon digital camera, some extra memory, and batteries.

He tried to take Aunt Morgan out to dinner, but she insisted on making Ryan a last home-cooked meal. "Don't know when you're going to get another one of these—eating all that dry gorb or whatever you call it, and squirrels, and rabbits, or whatever you—"

"It's not going to be like that. I don't expect to have to catch squirrels. I have plenty of jerky and there's towns along the way with restaurants."

"You mean you aren't going to be living off the land in the wilderness for five months?" she asked with her hand to her chest, like she was clutching her fear.

"No." Ryan smiled and gave her a hug.

***

It was Sunday, April 22, 2007, his parents wedding anniversary, *how right*, when he hopped the flight to San Diego, making it to Campo, California, along the Mexico border. He was late getting started, early April the usual start date for the 200 hikers attempting the feat each year, hoping to finish in September.

One other hiker camped out near him that night, a 40-something internet executive who was going to try to find himself on the PCT. Robert Winslow introduced himself. Out of shape and recently divorced, he showed Ryan pictures of his teenage boys he was going to impress with his accomplishment. Ryan smiled and wished him luck.

***

Ryan woke before the sun came up. Not waiting for Robert Winslow, he broke camp and packed up. He was surprised he spotted a dark bird circling above in the distance.

No, it couldn't be.

Ryan glanced behind him. He couldn't say why, but he felt as if someone or something was after him. He took off with determined strides.

18

RYAN

Three minutes without air. Three days without water. Three weeks without food. Ryan knew those were the limits of human existence. He carried 16 pounds of water, a third of the weight he hefted, in two one-gallon bladders tucked in his backpack. A tube protruded over his artificial shoulder so he could easily bring to his mouth to keep moving—and he needed to move—an urgency tugged him.

He tucked his long blond hair beneath a tan safari hat, wore matching khaki cargo pants, and a blue and red-striped rugby shirt. Ryan planned to change socks every day knowing the fastest way to slow down a hiker was to get blisters. He first major destination was 152 miles north to the Paradise Valley Café in Mountain Center, California, where he hoped to be in eight days. A juicy burger and an ice-cold beer waited for him there.

Eleven miles into his trek that first day, Ryan found a dried four-foot branch that he shaved into a smooth walking stick with his survival knife.

At mile 17, he visited the first of his many demons—recalling the letter he wrote Russell Stephens. Aunt Morgan was to read it in court the day the murderer was to be sentenced. He imagined her dressed in her Sunday best, gray hair up in a bun, holding the page in her trembling hands, voice cracking as she spoke his words.

Russell Stephens –

What you have done can't be undone. You must live with that. But know this…

I still feel my father's kind hand on my shoulder and remember the quiet moments we shared fishing on summer lakes with nothing but each other, mosquitoes, and fireflies for company. I can still taste my mother's sweet cooking, hear her soft voice, and feel her endless warm hugs. You can never take those from me.

You will receive a letter from me each year on the celebration of my parents' wedding anniversary—not their deaths. I will tell you what's become of their orphaned son … and hopefully, the man who becomes a loving husband and doting father. You can't take that away from me.

For the rest of your life, you will remember what you did on that day in 2004.

And I will try to forget.

Ryan Turner

By the second night, Ryan made it to Mount Laguna. He ate a beef and cheese burrito and two Golden Delicious apples he bought at the general store, leaning against the weathered siding of the building and letting his tightening muscles relax. He set up his tent a short ways away.

He replenished his water and was off at sunrise. He sighted a black bird circling ahead.

Is it you?

Five days later, Ryan walked into the Paradise Valley Café at 3:03 in the afternoon and dropped his backpack. Connie, a 40ish waitress smiled at Ryan, knowing the look of someone who'd been on the trail a while. She approached him as he stared at the menu mounted on the wall above the registers.

"What'll it be?" she asked with her pad and pen ready to take his order.

Ryan wrinkled his forehead and looked at her like she was speaking a foreign language.

"Why don't we start you with something to drink?" she asked and pulled out a chair for him to sit down.

Ryan plopped down and nodded. "Beer." He shook his head. "No, water." He paused then cocked his head. "Bring both."

A plate of fish tacos and two beers later, Ryan felt half human again. He waved Connie over. "Someplace nearby where I can take a shower and wash my clothes?"

"Not much here, but Idyllwild has everything. That's about a two-day hike from here." She handed him the bill. "Anything else? Maybe a slice of apple pie to go?"

Ryan shook his head. "Nope, that did me just fine."

***

Ryan did the 31.5 miles to Idyllwild in one day. Reaching the mile-high town was worth every step of it. He rented a cabin, went to the laundromat, and bought a small rotisserie chicken at the Village Market, licking his fingers long after the greasy salty mess was gone. While munching on a small bag of Cheetos in his room, he did the math—he was seven percent of the way to the U.S.-Canadian border.

Fifteen times more of what I just did and I'll be done. Then what?

He turned off the lights and fell into a deep slumber, his dreams tinged with the shadow of a crow circling above.

***

Most nights on the trail, if he had enough water and wasn't too tired, he fired up his camp stove and cooked up a just-add-water scramble to get something warm in his belly. Four days later he arrived at Big Bear Lake and went to the post office where a package waited for him. Clothes—socks, a pair of pants, and a few more shirts. It felt like Christmas. There was a note from Aunt Morgan that ended with, "Call or write me!"

Ryan sent a postcard to Aunt Morgan saying he was fine and wrote a letter to the VA.

Guys –

I logged 265 miles so far. I'm ten percent of the way. Feeling strong. No blisters. Almost ran out of water the last leg. Those of you who spent time in the middle east know what I'm talking about.

Next milestone: Wrightwood, about 100 miles away. If I hump it, could be there in four days—but I might take five or six—see more country—take some pictures. Rather than hike *through* it, I think I might like to hike *in* it.

Later, Ryan

It took Ryan six days to get to Wrightwood. Four of those days he didn't see another soul. Birds, insects, and small animals kept him company. Combined with his deep breath, they were the only melodies providing sweet rhythms to his strides. He felt alone, but not lonely, tired but not exhausted—at peace—something he hadn't had in a long time.

After that many days on the trail, even Ryan couldn't stand the smell of himself. A shower, laundromat, warm food, and a bed got him ready for the next day.

Ninety miles away Hiker Heaven waited for Ryan in Agua Dulce. The first two of his four days on the trail he spent hiking with a young couple from Oxnard, California. Christina and Bill were doing the PCT in sections whenever they got time off work. Ryan mostly listened to them talk about their work, their friends, and their families. He watched how easy they were with each other, the way they teased, touched and helped each other out, and how they laughed. A longing crossed Ryan's heart for a moment and he pushed it aside.

He didn't want to hear the usual condolences about his past, so he spoke about his mother and father as if they were still alive and he never went to war. It felt good. "I'm taking off a couple of semesters from Eastern Michigan to do this. Don't know when I'll get another chance once I graduate and join corporate America."

"You don't look like the corporate type," Christina said as her dark brown ponytail bounced from side to side with each step.

"Whatcha studying, Ryan?" Bill asked.

"I like the outdoors. Might major in forestry."

"Well, you've come to the right place," Christina said as she twirled around with her arms outstretched. She squinted at something ahead. "Hey, race you guys to the well!" She ran off.

Bill and Ryan glanced at each other and took off to catch her.

***

Jeff and Donna Saufley ran Hikers Heaven, a way station that accommodated up to 50 hikers—but only eight stayed the night Ryan visited. Water, food, inspiration, information, and laughter filled the air.

"For a thru-hiker, you're awfully late, by maybe three weeks," Donna said to Ryan around the campfire that night.

Ryan tossed a stick into the flames, "Yeah, well, you could say I'm making up for lost time."

Jeff spoke up, thoughtfully stroking his beard. "It can get nasty up in Washington and the Canadian border in late September and October."

"I can handle nasty," Ryan said with a grin.

Jeff looked Ryan over. "These mountains, they're relentless—been here forever—be here after we leave this planet. They don't care about us humans. We're like gnat farts to them. Can't see 'em, can't hear 'em, can't smell 'em."

"Speak for yourself, you old fart," someone called out from the dark.

After a good laugh, Ryan turned in.

***

It was 249 miles to the Kennedy Meadows General Store in Inyokern, California—Ryan's next stop. He figured it'd take 12 days if the weather held up. Another package would be waiting for him. Every morning before he started out, he took his knife and cut a small notch in his walking stick. He counted them up— 24 days so far. He sheathed his blade, looked up in the sky, and nodded at the black bird circling above.

How we doing?

***

Ryan spent an extra day looking for water, so it took 13 notches in his walking stick for him to make it to the general store. Christmas again waited for him. He prepared the packages in Kalamazoo before he left. The only thing Aunt Morgan had to do was seal the lid and mail them. This time she tossed in a box of Oreos.

"You're the best. 703 miles behind me. 1,857 more to go," he wrote on the postcard he sent her. "Next milestone, Red Meadows—200 miles away!" Ryan made sure to smear a little of the Oreo icing on the card.

***

At around the 145-mile marker of the next 200 miles, it started to rain—drizzles and mists at first, then big drops, small drops, downpours, wind so strong it even came at him sideways. The green poncho Ryan threw over his head and backpack flapped like laundry in a hurricane. By the end of the day he was soaked. Off the trail, he spotted a lean-to hikers probably built a few years back. Ryan lashed a tarp over it in the middle of the downpour.

He knew bodies lost heat 100 times faster in water than air, so he stripped down, dried off, and put on a change of dry clothes. Ryan shoveled a few handfuls of trail mix and granola in his mouth and curled up for a fitful night of sleep.

He woke to a loud "CAW" and grinned.

"What do you want?" he mumbled. Ryan stretched, untied the tarp covering the opening to the lean-to, and looked out. The rain had stopped, not even a mist, but the clouds were dark and heavy, like they weren't finished yet.

Another "Caw" got Ryan to pull on his boots and step out. He spotted the crow perched high up a pine. "What?" he asked it.

It hopped around on the branch.

Ryan walked ten feet from his tent, dropped his pants, and squatted. He was in the middle of a serious morning dump, when the crow let out a "Caw" again and turned its head towards the thick brush running up the mountainside. "CAW!"

"What's got into you?"

Ryan heard twigs snap and a low rumble. "Oh, shit," he said as he pulled up his pants. He ducked into the lean-to, grabbed his backpack and sleeping bag, and took off running.

A 100 yards later, as he rejoined the trail, he looked over his shoulder to see a black bear rip into the lean-to, tossing the make-shift dwelling aside like a kid opening Christmas presents. Ryan didn't stop running for a mile. The rest of the day he looked over his shoulder—and above, to thank the crow—but he never spotted it.

***

That night he was visited by other demons, this time from Afghanistan. What was left of LT Williams' face as he was taking a piss. Comms specialist Andrews on his back in the snow, a gurgling bloody hole in his neck. Nuñez in a hospital bed with vacant eyes, tubes and machines keeping him alive—without hope. Ryan sobbed himself to sleep.

19

RYAN

Four days later, with 47 notches on his walking stick, Ryan strode into Red Meadows Campground at Mammoth Lakes. The elevation was listed at an even 7,500 feet but Ryan hardly felt it, so used to the ups and downs after a month and a half on the trail. It was three in the afternoon, an hour before the deadline for putting in for a homemade dinner—and what a meal—salad, meatloaf, potatoes, ice tea, and apple pie.

With no laundromat, Ryan hand washed his clothes in the sink of his cabin, scrubbing them with bar soap, wringing them out, and doing it again. He strung the clothes over the shower rod. He scattered the care package from Aunt Morgan across the flowered quilt on his bed and he picked at the goodies she sent, this time a package of Fig Newtons and sour cherry gummy bears, his favorite.

He scrawled notes on two postcards—one for the vets and one for Aunt Morgan. He told the vets about the rain and the bear, and Aunt Morgan heard about the black bird who seemed to follow and watch over him. He asked her to send another tarp, shirt, and pants in the next package.

Ryan moved his laundry to a jury-rigged clothesline above the heater in his bedroom and tossed himself on the bed, a bone-deep weariness coming over him.

***

Next stop: Red Moose Inn, 295 miles away. It should take Ryan 15 days. Waiting for him would be baby back ribs barbecued over charcoal, fried potato wedges, beans, and carrots. It was a nippy 33 degrees when he opened the door to his cabin. Ryan notched day 48 on his walking stick, hefted his backpack, and headed back to the trail.

He ran into a few day hikers along the way and a group of four thru-hikers, two couples, who appeared to create their own problems. They fought blisters, a twisted ankle, not having enough water—but mostly each other. Ryan plodded along with them for a few hours, had lunch with them and took off. The peace of not hearing their shrill voices complaining about everything and everyone gave him a smile and quickened his pace.

He avoided the noise and people of Lake Tahoe and Truckee, staying to the trail. He looked for the crow for the 15 days and missed his watchful company. With 63 notches in his walking stick and 1,198 miles traveled, he rolled into the Red Moose Inn in Sierra City. A fresh set of boots, a new one-inch lift for his right leg, a tarp, a down vest, and more clothes were waiting to be picked up. Knowing how concerned Ryan was about the weight he carried, Aunt Morgan tossed in a bag of mini-marshmallows and some fruit roll-ups.

Ryan wrote two postcards again—the first thanking Aunt Morgan for her thoughtfulness and letting her know he was doing okay, but he missed her cooking. The one to the VA spoke of his quest and how he was even more determined to complete his journey to Canada. He challenged the vets to push themselves and show him what they could do when he returned.

***

Ryan looked at himself in the mirror the next morning, his clothes hanging loose on his six-foot, two-inch frame. *Must've lost 20 pounds.* He paused before he tossed his old boots into the trash. "You brought me a long way—through dust and rain, from deserts to mountains. Thank you, my friends. I won't forget you."

Old Station Fill Up was his next stop, 180 miles away. He stepped out onto the deck and cinched up his new boots. As always, he searched for his friend, the crow. Not finding him, he put another notch in his stick and headed out.

***

On the fifth day, Ryan made it to Little Haven in Belden, halfway to Old Station. He took a shower and tossed his clothes in the laundry. Donna, a young woman in tired jeans with short brown hair, stood by a handmade cardboard sign that offered haircuts for $10. She smiled at him. He took her up on it.

She led Ryan to a stump in the back of the camp. Her spirit was worn, beaten down by life. As she combed through his matted blond hair and began snipping, she started up. "Was living in Lancaster. Thought I'd be a beautician, even went to school for it. Got this nature bug thing, actually it was boyfriend Roy who got it—we aren't together any more. Anyway, he loved hiking and camping and all, went about 20 times. So, we decided to do the PCT. Broke up with me here in Belden, said I couldn't keep up with him, but I think it was something or someone else.

167

That was two years go…" She stood behind Ryan, paused, and pulled his head into her chest. She ran her fingers through his hair like what he imagined a lover would do.

"What—what are you doing?"

She stopped. "Sorry, I was just … it's been a while since someone like you came through here, and you're by yourself and all." She came around and stood in front Ryan and stared at him with brown eyes filled with loneliness and hope. "You seem real nice—and my tent, well, it's over there." She pointed to the woods at a dull green two-man tent with laundry strung on a line above it.

Ryan's mind filled with the face of Chelsea Wilkinson, his high school sweetheart and the awkward moments they spent fumbling with buttons and zippers in the back of his car—but ended up going nowhere. He shook his head slightly and whispered. "Just a haircut, Donna, if you don't mind."

She didn't say another word as she cut his hair. He gave her $50 when she was finished and he had to took away from her face that probably said, 'I'm not good enough for you either.'

For the next five days on the trail, he was haunted by her touch, the look she gave him, and the promise she held in her tent. A longing sprouted in him—to find a good woman to cherish.

***

On July 5th, Ryan cut the 74th notch in his stick at Old Station Fill Up. It was everything Ryan needed—hot meal, hot shower, and warm bed. He hand washed his clothes again and hung them to dry. Before turning in, he spread out his map on the floor of his cabin and traced the path he'd taken since leaving the Mexico border. His finger rested on one spot, some 55 miles before Red Meadows, where the crow warned him about the angry black bear.

Will I see you again, my friend?

He put the map away and went to bed—but his dreams were filled with the black bird as it flew above him belting out incessant "CAWS."

He woke before dawn and heard the crow outside. *You're back?* He jumped out of bed, threw on a jacket, and tiptoed outside the cabin into 20-degree weather. There on a rail sat the black bird—regal, wise, playful.

Ryan nodded his head in the direction of the bird. "What do you want?"

It thrust its head toward Ryan and let out another "Caw."

"Okay, okay. Gimme a minute and we'll get going."

Ryan left the cabin door open to check on the crow while he got dressed and packed. One last glance around his cabin, he hefted his backpack and headed out.

"Caw," the crow said again and took off heading straight for the trail.

You done this with other hikers?

Next stop: 284 miles to the Seiad Valley Post Office, only 10 miles from the Oregon border. He figured it'd take him 14 days to get there, maybe less, with good fortune and good weather. Another care package would be waiting for him. Ryan grinned wondering what Aunt Morgan would sneak in the box this time.

***

The crow kept Ryan company the entire way. The marshmallows were alright, but the peppered turkey jerky was the big hit. Halfway through their trek, the bird trusted Ryan enough to take food from his hand. "I think I'll call you Blackie—for obvious reasons."

***

Aunt Morgan must have read Ryan's mind. When they reached Seiad two weeks later, there were three extra packs of jerky and some apples in the care package. A soft bed, clean clothes, and Ryan was ready at dawn the next morning, and Blackie was waiting for him. "We'll be heading into Oregon today and be in Shelter Cove in 12 days."

Blackie tilted his head to the side and let out a "Caw."

"Okay. Let's go, Blackie."

***

On the third day, Ryan overtook three thru-hikers, buddies taking a year off of college to test their resolve and friendship— neither seemed to be working. Ryan noticed Blackie stayed away when other people were around and he was happy when he reappeared. The fourth day out, Ryan rigged a cup on top of his pack for Blackie to get a snack when he wanted. It was fun the way the black bird flew at him from the front and landed on his back, or surprise-attacked him from behind to peck at some jerky.

***

July 31, 100 days into his journey, Ryan arrived at Shelter Cove, got a cabin, did laundry, and sat down for a hot plate of stick-to-your-ribs diner food.

Stick-to-your-ribs—that's what you used to say, Dad.

Ryan wrote out his usual two postcards, saying his next stop was 243 miles away at Cascade Locks Ale House. "That's right," he wrote the vets. "I'm hiking all those miles for a cold beer. Should take 20 days, 18 if I'm extra thirsty."

Before going to bed, Ryan went outside to look around for Blackie. He found him perched high up in a tall pine outside his cabin. "Goodnight, my friend."

"Caw," Blackie croaked back.

***

Blackie kept Ryan company all the way to Cascade, playing their little game of nibbling on turkey jerky Ryan placed on top of his backpack. Whenever anyone else was within a quarter mile of them, Blackie took off, always flying out of sight until they left.

At night the temperature dropped well into the 20s, occasionally into the teens. It took them 26 days to make it to the Ale House, the last postal drop in Oregon. They would have made it sooner but Ryan took a wrong step and sprained his left knee halfway through their trek.

It was August 26rd and now there were 126 notches in his walking stick. His left knee was swollen but not so bad he couldn't continue. He'd come too far to quit now—and he felt an odd obligation to Blackie to keep going.

Aunt Morgan tossed in extra jerky in his care package after reading Ryan's last postcard about Blackie and his affinity for the salty, stringy meat. After a solid night's sleep in a cabin, Ryan swung his legs out of bed and when they hit the floor he winced, his left knee stiff and swollen. *I just need to warm it up.*

He took a step—a twinge of pain shot through his knee. He took another—better but not good enough to traverse the remaining 495 miles. He needed help. At the Columbia Market he found some. A few straggling hikers swore their remedy would work to reduce the swelling and pain.

"Advil, ice, and elevate," one said.

"Alternate between heat and ice every two hours for 24 hours," the other added.

Ryan bought the Advil and a heating pad, got a room for one more night, and filled up his ice bucket. He spent the day dozing, alternating between ice and heat, and watching old movies on TCM and getting caught up on news with CNN and ESPN. He missed a lot in four months. The Tigers were in second place, a game and a half behind Cleveland. George Bush couldn't run for a third term as president, so all sorts of candidates were being talked about including a black Senator from Chicago and Bill Clinton's wife, Hillary.

When he tested his leg out the next morning—it was better, but he could tell he wouldn't keep up the same pace as he'd done the past 2,155 miles. He took a strap off his pack and cinched it below his left knee. It felt sturdier. He found Blackie waiting for him when he opened the front door to his cabin.

"Hope you don't mind if we go a little slower."

"Caw," Blackie said and took to the sky.

It took three hours for them to reach the Bridge of the Gods over the Columbia River Gorge. Ryan spotted the three majestic southern volcanoes of Washington—Rainier, St. Helens, and Adams—no snow on them yet. He spotted Blackie. "This is the last time we're gonna be at this low of an elevation, but that doesn't make a difference to you, does it?" He bent down to cinch the strap below his knee, adjusted his backpack, and hobbled off.

His usual 20 miles a day, dropped to eight miles the first day, and seven the second. "It'll take 60 days as this rate," Ryan mumbled to himself. "White Pass Crackle Barrel Store, that's what's next—133 miles away." He spotted Blackie above him. "Let's get it in gear," he yelled.

***

It took Ryan 15 days to reach his destination and he struggled every step of the way. He stumbled into the White Pass Crackle Barrel Store on September 11th. A TV in the corner broadcast a retrospective on the six-year anniversary of the attacks on the World Trade Center in New York. When they got into the ensuing war—he had to leave.

Asleep that night in his cabin, Ryan dreamt of the faces of the 23 ragheads who would never breath again, all because he pulled a trigger. He bolted upright in bed—his sheets soaked with sweat—his face wet with tears. He limped to the bathroom, splashed water in his face, and looked in the mirror. He saw his father staring back at him—a man hollowed out by war. His father's words came back at him. "I know you thought about the military while you were working and saving for school—but that's a last option. War does things to a man—I should know."

Sorry I let you down, Dad.

He changed his clothes, went back to bed and tried to get some rest, but couldn't.

***

Saturday, September 15, 2007. Ryan had 347 miles to go and a left knee that wasn't cooperating. One last supply drop for the PCT, at Snoqualmie Pass Inn—only 99 miles away. It took 11 days to get there, Blackie urging him all the way—waking him in the morning and keeping Ryan going during the day. His last care package at Snoqualmie was full of surprises—37 of them—letters from the guys at the VA urging him on, telling him what they'd accomplished since he left them in April.

Ryan read each one of them—feeling the weight of the extra responsibility he created by involving them. *I gotta finish—or die trying.*

20

RYAN

September 17, 2007. The end of the Pacific Crest Trail was only 248 miles away, over the border in Canada. A swollen knee. A crow named Blackie urging him on. Aunt Morgan and 37 vets in Kalamazoo counting on him. He placed their letters under his gray Henley shirt next to his heart, a reminder of what they meant to him. Ryan's was fully loaded with supplies and obligations to last 25 days.

At his current pace, Ryan calculated he would finish somewhere around the middle of October and run into unsettling weather and nighttime temperatures in the teens—but he was prepared. One last hot homecooked meal at the Snoqualmie Pass Inn, one last warm bed, and two last postcards. Ryan left them at the front desk to mail.

A quarter mile down the trail, Blackie joined him, swooping down from behind to snag some turkey jerky. "Good to see you too," Ryan said and smiled as he hobbled down the well-marked trail.

During the next 13 days, he ran into a few day hikers, but no thru hikers as they were done for the season. When he woke up October 1st, he smelled snow. He poked his head out of his tent to find Blackie across from him on a branch. "It's coming, Blackie. I feel it in my left shoulder." He patted the artificial joint and grinned.

Blackie let out a "Caw" and took to the air. By midday it was flurries, by nightfall steady big flakes drifted silently to the ground where they slowly melted into the trail. Ryan pitched his tent near the trail, the opening away from the wind. He cooked up some trail food, supposed to be ravioli with a delectable lobster sauce. A small packet of artificial parmesan cheese added some taste to it. He needed the calories so he didn't mind. He had worse.

Ryan flashed back to his platoon in their barracks prior to their last mission in Afghanistan—guys trading for their favorite MREs—Nuñez looking for Pop Tarts. He smiled, then the image of Nuñez being kept alive by machines flooded his mind.

They pull your plug yet?

The names of the other guys were distant now, like something he once read in a book—Buzz, LT Williams, Ramirez with his dog, Andrews, Daniels the corpsman, Christian, Thompson, Polski, Vernon, Sanchez, Hollins and … the names and faces of the other 31 Marines faded like water running between his fingers.

Damn! Someone should remember.

Ryan slept uneasy and cold that night, not even the portable stove was enough to keep him warm.

***

Days to go: 12.

Miles to go: about 121.

It didn't get above 30 degrees for the next eleven days and the cold wouldn't leave him. The trail became treacherous, slippery after icy rains and hail—nothing like the sizes they talked about on the news, lemons or golf balls, more like peanuts. For every five steps Ryan took, it felt like he slid back one, not helping his left knee any. The only things good about completing those days was that Blackie was still with him—but even his "caws" sounded cold and tired.

***

Ryan's last morning on the trail. One heat-em-up meal remained, some kind of freeze-dried scrambled eggs with ham and peppers. He squatted by the stove and cooked it up, holding his hands out to catch any escaping heat. The stove sputtered the last bit of its fuel as he stirred the mess for the last time. Ryan ate the meal in his tent and shivered.

He took inventory as he packed for the last time. One unopened package of teriyaki turkey jerky remained along with some trail mix and granola. Plenty of water. He rolled up his pad and sleeping blanket, broke down his tent, and secured everything to his backpack. The lightest it ever was.

Ryan wore gloves, a beanie, a parka, and a poncho over it all. He grabbed his walking stick, noticing he stopped notching it sometime during the last month. He looked up through a nasty drizzle of sleet and snow and saw Blackie ruffle his feathers in disapproval. Ryan let out a "Caw" and Blackie gave him one back.

They started out.

***

Early that morning Ryan crossed the border into Canada, a trail marker indicating the boundary. As he plodded along, the temperature dropped, and the sleet turned to hail and freezing rain. Late that afternoon, with no one around to mark the occasion except Blackie, Ryan hobbled up to the five square logs jutting out of the ground. They were covered in a thick layer of ice. He could barely make out the inscriptions in the dusky light.

[Northern Terminus. Pacific Crest National Scenic Trail. 2627 Miles.]

There was no one to take pictures, no buddies to congratulate him, no father to slap him on the back—just Blackie. Ryan fumbled through his backpack to get his camera, placed a piece of jerky on the tallest marker, and Blackie flew to it like he knew he was going to pose. He clicked. Blackie let out a loud "CAW" as if to say 'we made it.' He clicked again.

"Now, time to go home," Ryan grinned and nodded with finality.

The icy rain grew in intensity, the ground under him slick as oil. Ryan put the camera away, grabbed his backpack by the handle and used it like a large cane to give him some stability, the walking stick in his other hand. He took cautious choppy steps—his breath coming out in gusts of steam. Off the trail in the dimming light, he spotted a small grove of trees about a hundred yards down an embankment and headed for it—good shelter. Blackie let out a "Caw."

"It's okay," Ryan called back.

Ryan wasn't 15 yards into his descent, when he slipped and found himself on his belly sliding on a blanket of ice with nothing to stop him. He grasped his backpack and shoved his hand inside, coming out with the ice axe he packed six months before. He heaved it into the hillside and it bounced off. As he picked up speed, Ryan let go of his backpack, placed both gloved hands around the axe, and swung down—no penetration but it scraped some and he slowed a little.

He passed the grove of trees and glanced down the hill where his backpack skidded unabated. Still sliding, Ryan inched up on his elbows and put all his weight on the ice axe—pointing the stainless steel tip against the icy slick surface. It squealed and scraped, Ryan sliding another 50 yards before coming to slow stop. He squinted into the murky gray. His backpack slid into the dark somewhere below him. Off to his right, an outcropping of boulders 30 yards away provided some cover, and to the left maybe something was 50 yards away, he couldn't tell.

He opted for the boulders. Keeping his belly to the icy ground and using the ice pick and whatever footing he could find, he inched his way. Night was upon him after the half hour it took to make it to the boulders. Ryan chipped away the ice at the base of the boulders to give himself some traction and a place to sit, all the while the icy sleet kept up its relentless assault.

He took some deep breaths and a few moments to center himself. His pants were soaked, his gloves wet, his poncho torn, he had no tent, but other than that he was okay.

Yeah, other than that.

Ryan shuddered. He needed to dry off, get some shelter, and some heat. No way to dry. No shelter other than the poncho. *Heat.* Inside his coat, he kept a lighter and a flashlight. Ryan found them and shined the flashlight onto his surroundings—no clear way to get off the slope in any direction. With his poncho flapping in the wind, he flicked the lighter, a fancy plasma one that could light anywhere. Heat, barely any, but heat.

Ryan searched in the dark looking for something to burn. Nothing. *The letters!* He took a glove off, unzipped his jacket and reached under his shirt, touching his skin. "Shit, that's cold."

He pulled out a handful of letters, wedged himself against the largest boulder. Using the poncho to deflect the sleet, Ryan pulled in his boots so that he curled his six-foot two-inch frame into a ball. He grabbed his lighter and sparked a flame that he put to a letter that he held. *Heat.* He rotated and tipped the paper over so that the flames spread evenly. When it was about to go out, he lit another letter and felt a surge of warmth. *Yes!*

For fifteen minutes, Ryan kept reaching in for more letters, until there were no more, the last one's amber edges turning into black ash that crumbled in his gloved hand and blew away. The heat gone, he pulled the poncho tight around him, his knees into his chest.

The freezing rain had stopped. Not a sound. Only the cold for company. It closed in on him like a lion on the hunt, but instead of fighting, he gave into it. Ryan closed his eyes, imagining what it must feel like to fall overboard into the cold Atlantic during the winter, tread water until you could move no more—and finally let go.

No more death.

No more pain.

No more memories.

No more trying.

Only quiet sleep.

He felt the cold calling to him with its sweet words. *Let go. Let go.*

He did.

21

RYAN

A distance voice called, "Here you come. Ryan. Ryan Turner!" Like his mother did when he was a kid and he didn't want to come in from playing. His lips parted in a smile with the memory. Someone smacked his hands and rubbed them. Mixed with the voice was a rhythmic beep. Everything smelled clean and fresh.

He wrinkled his forehead.

Where am I?

He slowly blinked his eyes open and squinted.

"There now. You gave us quite a scare," said a woman with dark hair in a light blue smock.

"Where..." Ryan's voice faded.

"You're in Fraser Canyon Hospital—in Canada. Some folks found you in that nasty ice storm and brought you here. You were suffering from hypothermia and exposure. They said something about a black bird showed them where you were."

"Blackie?" Ryan croaked.

"Were you with someone else?"

"No. My crow, the bird. His name is Blackie."

"Is he your pet?"

"No. Well, sort of." He paused and blinked his eyes wider. "Where am I?"

"I'm Dorothy Callahan, your nurse. You're in Fraser Canyon Hospital—in Canada."

Ryan's eyes fluttered closed and he let out a deep warm breath.

***

Ryan spent three days in the hospital getting warm and putting on a few pounds. On the fourth morning there was a light knock on the door. A 40ish man in a white coat came in.

"Hey, doc," Ryan said with a smile.

The doctor stepped to the foot of Ryan's bed, picked up his chart, and scanned it quickly. "A hundred fifty pounds on your frame is too little," Dr. Bochler said as he pushed his reading glasses back up his nose. "Your bloodwork showed inordinate amounts of protein. What have you been eating?"

Ryan scooted up in bed to a sitting position while the doctor placed a stethoscope on various places on his chest and back like they'd done half a dozen time before, Ryan breathing deeply. "Mostly turkey jerky and trail food."

"Well, you've come a long way since we got you." The doctor scribbled some notes on Ryan's chart. "I'm going to recommend discharging you this morning, but no outdoor activities for a couple of months, especially in cold weather. Got it?" He wagged at finger at Ryan.

Ryan nodded and smiled. "Yes, doc."

***

Ryan took two buses and the rest of the day to get to Bellingham, Washington. He checked into a Holiday Inn without any luggage, just the clothes he wore to the hospital. He got the key to room 723. Clean, bright, two double beds. He went to the window and looked out, the city streets and buildings looking so foreign after six months in the wild.

Where'd you go, Blackie?

As he reminisced, another important name in his life jumped into his mind.

Aunt Morgan.

He called her and told her he was fine—but said nothing about his hospital stay. "I'm thinking of renting a car and driving back to Kalamazoo, but taking my time—seeing some of the country from the road."

"The men at the VA have been asking about you. They were worried. So was I," Aunt Morgan said with a sniffle.

"I was worried too. But everything's okay now." Ryan paused, his voice choking up, recalling that freezing night when their letters gave him hope and warmth for 15 minutes. "You'll never know how much their letters meant to me."

"Well, you'll just have to tell me all about when you get back here."

***

The next morning, Ryan rented a hardtop red Jeep Wrangler, just the kind of vehicle to drive east during the winter. The rental office gave him a map and he traced out his trip through Washington, Idaho, Montana, South Dakota, Minnesota, Wisconsin, Illinois, Indiana, and finally Michigan. He'd take I-5 south to the 405 and catch the I-90 east out of Bellevue. He had all the time in the world. It was 2,274 miles to Kalamazoo—such a small number after hiking the PCT.

He stopped by a Target to buy a duffle bag, toiletries, some clothes, a Detroit Tigers hat, and a cooler. The Safeway supermarket was his next destination—lots of fruits and vegetables, some juices, plus some Fig Newtons and jerky. When he got out to his car, he found himself looking up in the trees, half expecting Blackie to swoop down and get some jerky.

I miss you.

***

Ryan's first day on the road was six hours long and ended with a stop in Coeur d'Alene, Idaho. It was odd—he had all the time in the world but he felt a subtle urgency pulling him east. He rented an off-season cabin on a lake, had a meal at a local diner, and a good night's sleep.

In the morning, he poured a cup of instant coffee in his room and walked down to the water's edge in 20-degree weather. Clear. Calm. A boat in the middle of the lake held two fishermen.

A loud "Caw" startled him and he almost slipped into the lake. He looked up in nearby trees for the source of the sound. "Blackie!" he called out. Nothing. "Blackie!" he yelled.

"Caw" came from behind him. Ryan turned to find Blackie walking back and forth on the rail by his cabin, like an expectant father awaiting the birth of his first child. "Caw," he let out again.

"I know," Ryan answered with the grin as he walked towards the bird, "I missed you, too. Now, let's get going."

22

Ryan topped off his tank and merged onto the I-90 heading east. Large 18-wheelers filled the interstate spewing their black diesel exhaust out of polished chrome pipes. Dotted in between them were businessmen driving rental sedans, ranchers in pickups, and then there was Ryan. They all had destinations, purpose, places to go, people to visit—someone to love.

Where am I going?

A familiar feeling came over him—like when he got out of the VA hospital—no direction, lost, alone. But it was different this time. There was a peace and calmness, like he left his confusion and hatred somewhere on the PCT hiking those 2,650 miles and almost dying. He rolled down the window and looked up ahead, the wind nearly blowing off his Detroit Tigers hat, and spotted Blackie flapping his wings.

Where I should go now?

***

Around eleven, Ryan pulled off the interstate in Butte, Montana—gassed up and found his way to a Denny's. Before he we went in, he glanced up hoping to spot Blackie, but knew his habit of staying away from other people.

See you soon.

He grabbed The Crested Butte local newspaper from a rack inside the restaurant. The aroma of the hot grill had Ryan salivate for a Grand Slam—scrambled eggs, both sausage and bacon, home fries, pancakes, and hot black coffee. Lots of calories but he needed to put on weight. He took a seat at the counter where Doreen, a 50-something waitress with tattoos and angry dark hair, took his order.

Everything about the paper made Ryan smile. Butte, Montana—about half the size of Kalamazoo but with mile-high elevation. He read the news about the local school board, minor arrests, and reports that the Bulldogs' high school football team had lost eight games in a row, so no playoffs this year. The paper was filled with ads—three car dealers trying to outdo each other with Halloween weekend sales of outgoing 2007 models, a mortuary, grocery stores, and a few other local businesses.

The classifieds caught Ryan's attention with their quirky items for sale and personals. A man interested in buying three bear traps was also looking for a companion. "Must enjoy skinning animals and whiskey. Any age and extra pounds okay." Ryan chuckled.

Doreen came by with a refill and he watched her walk away.

What kind of woman would I advertise for? Kind. Great smile. Good cook. Tender lover, whatever that is. Must like the outdoors and want children—might even have some.

"A Good list," he mumbled.

It was one o'clock when Ryan checked into the Super 8 Motel, went to his room, flopped on the bed and flicked on the TV. The Lions were playing the Bears, a crucial game especially because they were division rivals. The game ended with the Lions on top 16-7 and sporting a 4-2 season record.

Maybe this is your year?

A bite to eat at a local pub and Ryan hit the rack early.

***

As Ryan pulled onto the interstate just after seven in the morning, he spotted Blackie again, high above and ahead.

Where we going now, my friend?

Ryan had a choice to make at Billings, either take the I-94 and head north to go through North Dakota, or stay on the I-90. Blackie made the decision for him, even leading Ryan to a turnoff from I-90 at Crow Agency an hour later. He needed gas anyway. Blackie stayed nearby in a tree watching Ryan fill up.

What you up to now?

Before Ryan pulled out of the Crow Nation Express gas station, Blackie let out a "caw" and took off. Ryan followed him down an access road running alongside the I-90, finally turning east onto Route 212.

Now what?

A mile down the road, Blackie landed atop the Custer Battlefield Trading Post. Ryan parked, got out of his red Wrangler, and looked up. "Is this where you want me to go?"

Blackie let out a loud "Caw."

"Okay, I get it. I'm hungry anyway." Ryan glanced at his watch, *11:45.*

Ryan tipped his Detroit Tigers hat to Blackie and went inside—alert, an anxiousness teasing him—something he hadn't felt in a long time. Scents of rawhide and dusty trail mixed with the café's aromas. Ryan took in the souvenir shop with its collectibles, fascinated by their cradleboard collection, and all the books on Custer's Last Stand in 1876 at the Battle of Little Big Horn. He was busy reading the opening pages to *A Terrible Glory*, when a voice interrupted him.

"You might want to take a look at *Lakota Noon*—it gives the natives side of the story."

Ryan turned to find a beautiful young woman with long dark hair holding a book. She wore traditional Indian buckskin outfit and her name badge read 'Kay.' He took the book and nodded a quiet, "Thanks, Kay." His stomach growled.

"You might want to get something at the café, too," she said with a grin.

Ryan blushed. "You heard that, too?"

"Yes."

He placed the other book back on the shelf and held up her book. "Where do I pay?"

"I'll take it at the register. And, if you don't like it, you can exchange it for something else." She wandered towards the register.

"I'm putting a lot of trust in your recommendation," he said placing the book on the counter.

"Trust has to be earned." She nodded.

Ryan pulled out his wallet. "Since I'm taking your advice for reading material, is the café any good?"

"Well," she said taking his charge card, "it's famous for the Crow Indian Taco, but if you're really hungry, you ought to try the Buffalo steak."

He wrinkled his forehead and tilted his head. "Buffalo?"

"You must not be from around here." She handed him the charge slip to sign.

Ryan signed and looked up. "Kalamazoo—in Michigan." He held up his hand and pointed to a spot on his palm. "It's about here."

"Where?"

"Oh, it's the shape of the state, it's called the Michigan Mitten—kinda shaped like a hand. Kalamazoo's right about here."

Kay cocked her head and handed him a receipt. "That's funny. What brought you here?"

Ryan paused and whispered, "A crow."

"An Indian?"

"No, a bird. I've been following him, or he's been guiding me. All the way from Mexico to Canada. And even before that. He landed on your building."

"Oh, come on now." She squinted to see if he was joking. "You've got to show me."

"Okay." Ryan led her outside and they looked up. There was Blackie, walking on the roof's peak, preening as if waiting for a photo opportunity. "See," Ryan pointed.

Blackie let out a loud "Caw" and flapped his wings, staying in place.

Kay shook her head. "Well, I'll be. But I hate to disappoint you—that's not a crow—it's a raven."

"No way."

"Yes, crows are much smaller."

"Sorry about that, Blackie," Ryan called up to the bird.

A man in the trading post window tapped on the glass and motioned to Kay. She started for the front door. "Gotta go. Tell me how your meal was?"

"Sure." Ryan looked up at Blackie again.

So, you're a raven.

Blackie let go a "Caw," flapped his great wings, and took off heading south. Ryan watched him for a few minutes until he was just a speck.

Is that it? Will I ever see you again, my friend?

***

After the buffalo steak, he went back to the gift shop to thank Kay. A young blond boy, in a gray T-shirt, jeans, and sneakers, ran around the store touching everything, picking up souvenirs.

A 50ish Indian with a graying pony tail, the man who tapped on the window, spoke to Kay in a corner. "Just look at him," he glared a blond boy. "Nothing Crow about him. You know he's not to be in here while you're working."

"I'm sorry, Mr. Graytree. My sitter got sick and she just dropped him off. And his name is Easton."

The manager put his hands on his hips. "That's not even a Crow name." He shook his head. "Look, he's not allowed in here unattended. Either he leaves or you both go—makes no difference to me."

Easton ran over to Ryan and stopped directly in front of him, looking up. "Hey, mister."

Ryan bent down to Easton's level. "Hey back at you, little fella," Ryan said.

The boy threw his arms around Ryan's neck, gave him a tight hug, then went to explore the store.

Ryan reeled from the unexpected affection and looked to Kay.

Kay missed the exchange, instead glancing at her watch. "Look, I've only got an hour left on my shift. He won't make any trouble. I promise."

"See that he doesn't. And if anything breaks, you pay for it, understand?" the manager wagged his finger at Kay.

"Yes."

Ryan watched the manager storm out of the gift shop, but not before he glowered in Easton's direction.

Jerk.

Kay went to Easton and knelt down, taking trinkets out of his hand, and putting them back on the shelves. She took him firmly by the shoulders to get his attention. "Easton, look at Ah-chee."

He obeyed and stared at her with his round blue eyes.

"You have to stay next to me. No running around. Can you do that for Ah-chee? I'll take you for strawberry ice cream if you do," she bargained.

Easton's eyes sparkled. "Yes, Ah-chee." He took her hand and walked behind the counter where he sat on a small chair. Kay handed him a book and crayons.

Ryan was overwhelmed by the simple exchange—but there was something else—he couldn't put his finger on it. He approached the counter.

Kay looked up surprised. "So, come back to exchange the book?"

Ryan shook his head. "No."

"You come to complain about the meal?" she grimaced.

Ryan patted his belly and shook his head again. "No." He grinned. "I wanted to thank you for the recommendations." He leaned in and whispered, "And I didn't like the way your manager talked to you about your boy."

"Oh, that's okay. If Easton looked more Crow it probably wouldn't be a problem."

Ryan took at quick peek at her left hand and noticed no wedding ring. "I got nowhere to go—if you want, I'll keep him occupied until you get off work."

Kay looked him over. "No, that's okay. But thanks."

Ryan glanced down at his clothes and wondered how he must look to her—tall, thin, long blond hair sticking out a Detroit baseball cap, jeans, long-sleeve shirt. "I know how little boys are. He'll get tired of coloring in five minutes—then he'll be a handful."

"How do you know? You have kids?"

"I was once his age—over 20 years ago." Ryan grinned. "Anyway, I'll be over by the window reading my book if something changes."

"Okay." She watched Ryan move to the window, then looked down at Easton.

The door pinged with a new customer and Kay moved from behind the counter to help them.

***

Somewhere during Kay's time with yet another customer, Easton slipped out from behind the counter and found his way onto Ryan's lap. She heard her boy giggle and spotted him with

193

Ryan. She was about to say something, but instead snuck up behind them to listen, standing behind a display of Indian jewelry.

Ryan read the back cover of his book in an animated voice, "…to describe events in meticulous detail." Ryan looked at Easton. "Do you know what *meticulous* means?"

Easton shook his head, looking up at Ryan.

"Well, little man, it means—let me see—meticulous means very precise." Ryan grinned.

Easton had a blank look on his face.

"Uh, I see. Well, precise means very—it doesn't matter— meticulous is just another big word." Ryan poked Easton and they laughed.

Kay cleared her throat and stepped out from behind the display. "So, there you are."

Easton stopped laughing and bowed his head, expecting to get in trouble.

"He's not bothering you, is he?" she asked.

"No. Just the opposite. He's the perfect companion—he likes to hear me talk." Ryan tilted his head to the side and nodded his head. "It's been a while."

"Since you spoke to a three-year old?" Kay chuckled.

"No, since I had a real conversation. Talked to the crow— uh, the raven, for six months while hiking the PCT."

"What's that?"

"The Pacific Crest Trail—all two thousand six hundred fifty miles of it."

Kay's mouth hung open. "You did that?"

"Yes." Ryan stood. "I'll tell you all about it if you let me take you both for some strawberry ice cream—my treat."

Kay glanced at her watch. "My shift ends at two, in ten minutes. Got to tally the register, then we can go." She bent down to Easton. "Would you like that, to have some strawberry ice cream with…" she looked at Ryan.

"Ryan Turner—from Kalamazoo, Michigan."

"Ryan Turner," Kay said to Easton.

Easton bobbed his head in approval. "Stawburry ice ceam!"

23

K ay said to Ryan, "There's a Dairy Queen in Hardin. Not that far, if you want to follow us." She walked out of the trading post holding Easton's hand.

"Sounds perfect, as long as they have strawberry ice cream," Ryan said.

Easton looked over at him. "Stawburry ice ceam!"

Ryan and Kay shared a smile and hopped in their cars, Ryan waiting while she put an excited Easton in his car seat before they pulled out.

Fifteen minutes later they took their ice cream to a table by a window. Easton dug in right away, the sweet strawberry topping dribbling off the sides of his spoon.

Kay quickly tucked a napkin over his gray sweatshirt.

"My mother used to do that with me, too," Ryan said.

"Always on the lookout for potential disasters," Kay said. "He can be a handful." Her eyes landed on Ryan. "Now, you're supposed to tell us all about your hiking and the raven."

Ryan told them about notching his walking stick every day, Aunt Morgan shipping care packages, the raven, people he met, the towns he passed through, his small adventures. He kept it so interesting, Easton stopped eating and listened with his mouth open, his ice cream melting. When Ryan got to the part about the rain and the bear, Easton's blue eyes widened.

"Was the bear mad?" Easton asked.

"No. Probably just hungry—like you were for strawberry ice cream," Ryan answered. "Hey, you got some left."

"More bird, more bird," Easton demanded.

Ryan went on to describe how he saw the same bird in Afghanistan, in the hospital in Germany, Walter Reed in Maryland, in Kalamazoo, and at the start of the PCT. He left out the rifle range and the courtroom steps. "It's almost like he was saying 'you're in the right place—now, follow me.'"

"You're joking, right?" Kay asked.

Ryan shook his head. "I know it sounds crazy."

"It could be something more," Kay said squinting her eyes.

"That raven saved my life more than once." Ryan looked out the window, his eyes moistening.

"Watcha lookin' at?" Easton asked.

Ryan turned to him. "Just remembering is all. Just remembering."

Kay reached over and placed a kind hand on Ryan's arm. "You know, Crow folklore speaks a lot to the spiritual connection with nature and humans. Maybe it was something more like that."

Ryan looked at her hand and back at her, their eyes fixed on each other until Easton interrupted. "More bird!"

Kay patted Ryan's arm lightly and withdrew her hand.

"Okay, now. Where was I? Oh yes, the raven." Every time Ryan used the word *adventure* in his story, Easton would chime in, "Venture." It became a game with them, Ryan coming to a point in his tale when he'd tap his fingers on the side of his temple and squint like he was trying to remember the word, and Easton would yell out, "Venture!"

Ryan would nod and say, "That's right" and continue.

***

It was after four o'clock when Ryan finished talking, both Kay and Easton transfixed the whole time.

Kay leaned in. "I've never seen him sit so still for so long."

Ryan shrugged his shoulders. "Must be the bears and birds."

Kay reached over, tousled Easton's hair, and pulled him in for a hug. "He's a good boy."

"If you don't mind me asking, where's his father?" Ryan asked.

"He, uh, passed away before Easton was born." She looked down at her boy. "It's just us two now."

"Well, I told you all about me—at least about my hike— but I don't know anything about you…" he left his words to float in the air.

"Not much to tell, really."

"I'd like to know more, if that's okay?"

"Have you ever been in California?"

"When I hiked the PCT. Oh, and MCRD for basic training."

"Where's that?"

"San Diego."

"Oh." Concern crossed Kay's face like a shadow. She grabbed her purse, slid out of the booth, and stood waiting for Easton. "Well, it's really been nice meeting you, Ryan." A twinge of sadness crossed her face. She turned to Easton. "Come now, time to go home."

Ryan got out of the booth, but Easton wouldn't budge.

Kay gave Easton a mother's stare. "Come on, I said." Still he wouldn't move. "Do you want me to count to five?"

Easton lowered his head and crawled out of the booth, stomping his feet on the floor.

"Sorry about that. Must be the sugar—"

Easton threw his arms around Ryan's legs in a desperate hug.

Kay reached to pull him away, saying to Ryan, "I'm so sorry. He's never done anything like this before."

Easton wouldn't let go.

Ryan patted him on the head and bent down. "It's okay. Everything's going to be okay, Easton. Ah-chee needs to take you home now."

"I wanna stay," Easton moaned.

Kay knelt down too. "Easton, you can't stay at Dairy Queen for the rest of your life. It's time to go home. Now, come along." As she grabbed hold of his hand, she looked at Ryan, and blushed.

A few moments passed. Ryan reached out for Easton's other hand. "Let's get you home, Easton, okay?"

Easton nodded and they walked out the Dairy Queen hand-in-hand, Easton in the middle, looking up at Ryan and then his mother with a big smile on his face.

Ryan lifted Easton into his car seat and tried to buckle him up, fumbling with the multiple snaps. Kay leaned over and clicked him in. "It's easy once you've done it a thousand times." Kay smiled, then it faded, and she crossed her arms. "Do you know a high society lady named Linda from the San Diego area?"

Ryan cocked his head, searching his memory, then shook it. "No."

Kay let out a small sigh, reached out her hand, and Ryan took it. In a tender voice she said looking in his eyes, "It was a pleasure meeting you, Ryan Turner." She paused. "It's too bad you live in Kalamazoo."

"Zoo, zoo," Easton beamed and cooed over and over.

They both look at Easton and grinned.

"I don't *live* there. I have a place in my Aunt's home." Ryan still held Kay's hand and she didn't try to pull away. "I'd like to see you—and Easton again—if that's okay."

She looked into Ryan's blue eyes, nodded slightly, and whispered words she thought she'd never say again, "Me too."

Ryan grinned. "That's great. What days do you have off?"

"Mondays and Tuesdays."

"If it's alright, I'll drop by Sunday afternoon at your job and see what works for you—or if you changed your mind."

"Could I ask you something, though—but you have to promise not to get offended." Kay said with concern in her eyes.

"Sure."

"Could I see your identification?"

Really?

"Of course." Ryan pulled out his wallet, took out his Michigan driver's license and VA card, handing them to her.

She looked them both over. "So, your birthday's in early June. You a Gemini?"

"I'm at the tail end, but yes." He paused and then ventured, "Is that okay?"

"Yes. And to answer your question, no, I won't change my mind." Kay smiled and handed him his ID. "What are you doing for the weekend?"

Ryan shrugged his shoulders. "See some of Montana? Any suggestions?"

"Drop by tomorrow morning for breakfast—it'll be busy— I'm working in the café but I'll have something for you."

***

Ryan checked into the Lariat Motel in Hardin, Montana— rustic, very western, but most important, not too far from the Custer Battlefield Trading Post. He had a smile full of memories of Kay and Easton—and purpose—for at least one more day when he'd see Kay.

One day at a time.

He didn't ask where Kay and Easton lived or for her phone number—he could tell she was uncomfortable with anything more. With the TV on in the background, he fell asleep and dreamt of bears and birds—and a little blond boy.

***

"What can I get you to drink?" Kay asked with a smile.

Ryan sat in a seat at the counter, a menu open. "Coffee. Black," Ryan answered and matched her expression.

He watched Kay drift to the coffee station, pick up the pot and a mug and head back, but not before she topped off a couple of customers along the way.

"Have you thought about what you'd like?" she asked while pouring his coffee.

"A recommendation."

"Well, if you like spicy, the breakfast burrito's good."

He leaned in so no one else could hear him. "I meant, where to go for the next couple of days."

"Okay, one breakfast burrito," she replied and noted it on her check and went to put in the order.

Out of the corner of his eyes he could tell all the patrons, especially the men, were watching her.

Oh, you don't want them to know.

***

After he finished his breakfast, Kay gave him the check. "They'll take care of this at the register." Her eyes told him she wanted to say more.

"Tell the chef he makes a mean burrito," Ryan said and nodded as he got up. He wandered over to the cashier and looked down—that's when he realized Kay gave him two pieces of paper. He paid the cashier, leaving a healthy tip and walked outside. He got in his Wrangler and looked at the note.

[Try the Little Big Horn Battlefield National Monument. It's a great hike—nothing like the one you went on—with a self-guided tour. Stop by tomorrow morning if you want another suggestion.]

Ryan couldn't stop grinning and as he drove to the site and couldn't wait until breakfast the next day.

***

Kay was right, the national monument was incredible. After reading *Lakota Noon*, he took in the battlefield and the exhibits from a different perspective. He hiked past where the exhibit ended and spent the day exploring, glancing up in the sky for Blackie and finding nothing. He was disappointed but somehow knew Blackie's job was finished. He came back to his hotel at dinner time with a new appreciation for the plight of Native Americans.

Ryan had a bite to eat and went back to his room. He stood by the window looking out when he called Aunt Morgan.

"Ryan, it's so good to hear from you. How far away are you?" There was excitement, as always, in her voice.

"I'm in Montana, a little town called Hardin. There's something…" he didn't know quite how to tell her as he fiddled with the draw cord on the cowboy-themed yellow curtains.

"What is it?"

"You know that crow I told you about?"

"Yes."

He told her about following the crow, now a raven, to a café and souvenir store on an Indian reservation.

"And…?"

"I'm going to stay here a bit—at least a week—see where things … how things go. I'll keep in touch."

"You sound awful mysterious, Ryan."

Ryan grinned. *Mysterious. That's a good way to put it.* "It's a mystery to me, too."

"Well, you take care now, you hear?"

"Always, Aunt Morgan."

24

Ryan stood outside the Trading Post Café doors shuffling his feet and rubbing his hands together to fight off the brisk morning air. He looked at his reflection in the glass—no baseball cap, just his mop of blond hair, a new wool plaid shirt, jeans, and hiking boots. His clothes hung loosely on him. He shrugged his shoulders.

It'll have to do.

The lock clicked and the door opened a crack. Ryan was greeted by Kay's bright smile peeking out. "You must be hungry." She swung the door wide open. "Come on in."

He stepped in timidly and looked around. "Who's here?"

"Just me and the chef. It's usually slow first thing. The busboy and other waitress come in at nine." She moved towards the counter and nodded at Ryan to follow. "Take a seat and tell me all about yesterday."

Ryan plopped onto one of the red vinyl seats and picked up a menu.

She plucked it away from him with a tease. "You won't need that. Just tell me what you feel like eating and the chef'll cook it up."

"Okay." He took a deep breath. "Let me see. How 'bout four eggs, sunny side up, extra crispy hash browns, four sausages, toast, sourdough if you have it, and plenty of coffee?"

"Must've been one heck of a hike yesterday," Kay said as she grabbed a pot of freshly-brewed coffee.

"It was, but I've got to put on at least twenty-five pounds."

She put down a mug and poured his coffee.

Ryan took a sip. "Oh man, this is good."

"It's the chicory."

"What's that?"

"It comes from a plant. They use the roots, grind them up, and roast 'em—add it to the coffee. Nice, huh?"

"Yeah." He took another sip.

"Let me get your order in before more customers arrive."

Kay turned to the pass-thru, scribbled down Ryan's order, stuck it in the silver order wheel, and yelled, "Charlie, got a special—and he's hungry."

"Got it, Kay," came a voice from the kitchen as the wheel spun around.

She moved back to the counter, leaning on it with attentive dark eyes. "So, tell me all about yesterday."

***

Ryan finished his story just as a ding came from the chef and a huge platter appeared in the pass-thru.

"Food's up." Kay turned and picked up Ryan's order just as two customers walked in. She set down his plate and whispered, "I'm glad you had fun yesterday."

She left to wait on of the new customers while Ryan dug into his breakfast.

***

Kay placed Ryan's check on the counter with a note for a suggestion for sightseeing. Along with it she wrote, [I get off at 2. Meet me in the parking lot then if you want]. He stared at it a moment, his heart swelling with a sweet anxiousness, like a moment of great importance was taking place but if he said the wrong thing it might disappear.

Kay added, "Easton can't stop talking about your black bird."

Ryan looked up at Kay. He grinned and nodded as he stood up. "I'd like to tell him more." He placed cash on the counter. "See you later," he whispered and headed for the door, new purpose taking hold of every step.

***

Ryan was in the parking lot by one-thirty and didn't spot Kay's car, but he waited. At two-fifteen he went inside, didn't see Kay, and asked a waitress, "Is Kay here?"

"Oh," a look of concern washed over her face. "She left around eleven, something about her boy being sick."

Ryan went back to his car and stared at the note with Kay's phone number. He called but it went to voicemail. "Hey, it's me, Ryan. I heard about Easton—that he's sick. I hope you're both okay. Anything I can do…" He hung up. A strange, deep worry tugged at him as he waited in his car.

Twenty minutes later, Kay called back. "Sorry about not being there. I'm in the ER—in the waiting room. They're doing all kinds of tests on Easton." He heard her stifle a sob.

"Where are you?"

"Crow-Northern Cheyenne Hospital."

"I'm coming." It took Ryan ten minutes to get directions and drive over there. He rushed in the emergency room doors and spotted Kay in the corner of the waiting room, head down, dabbing her eyes.

He sat next to her and placed a hand on her back. When she looked up at Ryan, she burst into deep sobs and buried her head in his chest.

Between Kay's tears, she told Ryan what the doctors believed was wrong with Easton. "I thought he was just having another dizzy spell. Then they said his weight loss indicated something else. They think it's, it's … maybe a rare blood disease," she whispered as if saying it any louder would make it more real.

"He'll be okay. They have treatments for everything now." He held her hands. "I haven't known you that long, but I'll help you get through this."

Kay looked into Ryan's blue eyes, a spark of hope in knowing she wasn't alone softened the moment.

A doctor walked up. "Miss Goodtree?"

Kay looked up.

"You can see your boy now. Follow me."

Kay turned to Ryan. "I'll be right back."

***

Kay returned to the waiting room thirty minutes later, shuffling over to Ryan as if every step was an effort. She sank into the seat next to him. He noticed a bandage on her arm.

He took her hands. "What did they say?" he asked.

She looked down. "He has … Easton's white blood count is dangerously low."

"They can fix it, can't they?"

"Yes, but…" her words faded with her hope.

"But what?"

"They're keeping him here for observation—he's asleep now." She tried to shake her head clear. "I've got to get some of his things from home."

"I'll go with you, anything to help."

"They took my blood to test if…" Kay looked up at Ryan her eyes welling with tears. "I don't know what I'll do if…"

"One thing at a time. Now, let's get his things. I think I should drive." Ryan stood and held out his hand.

She stood and took it. "I have to be there when he wakes up."

He nodded. "We'll make it quick."

On the twenty-minute drive to her home, she looked out the window and recounted some of the simple joys she experienced with Easton. "He has the kindest heart—like helping the younger kids at preschool tie their shoes or put on their jackets. At his preschool and church, the children call him Eaten because they can't pronounce his name." She turned to Ryan and smiled wearily. "Also, I think it's because he gives them the treats I pack for his lunch."

Ryan chuckled. "I used to do that."

"They had treats in Kalamazoo when you were a kid?"

"It's not another planet, although sometimes it feels that way."

Kay pointed to the exit. "Oh, turn off here."

***

On the drive back to the hospital, Ryan felt compelled to say, "I don't want you to think I'm crazy, or a stalker or anything, especially since I followed a black bird all the way from Afghanistan to the Custer Battlefield Trading Post—but I believe I'm here, in your life—and Easton's for a reason."

Kay reached over and took his hand. "I can't explain it but I feel it too." She took a deep breath and let it out. "I've only known one man in my life, my late husband. He was a gentleman when we were dating. When we married, in fact the day before we married, he turned into a monster." She paused. "I shouldn't say this, but I was glad when he died."

Ryan squeezed her hand to let her know it was alright and to continue.

"Well, as you can see, I don't have a very good track record with trusting men, even though it was only one."

"I don't have any track record with women except a girl I dated for a while in my senior year of high school. My dad taught me how to treat women. I saw the way he was with my mother."

"You never said much about them. You have any brothers or sisters?"

"No. And … and my parents, they were murdered."

Kay squeezed Ryan's hand. "Murdered?"

"Yeah." His eyes began to well up. He sat up and nodded his head at the road in front of them. "Hey, we're here." He pulled into the hospital parking lot and turned off the engine. They sat for a few moments not wanting to break the closeness honesty brings.

Ryan opened his door and gave Kay's hand one last squeeze. "Let's see how our little man's doing."

***

Ryan spent the night in a waiting room chair.

Kay stayed with Easton, trying to sleep in a chair next to his bed. He woke during the night scared not knowing where he was. Kay calmed him and brushed his hair out of his eyes, explaining what was going on as simply as she could.

"You know how you get dizzy sometimes?"

He nodded his head, worry in his eyes. "Yes."

"Well, the doctor thinks that maybe something in my blood can help you. Isn't that nice?"

"Ah-chee always helps."

"Yes, I do."

His eyes filled with tears. "But will Ah-chee die if you give me your blood?"

Kay smile and caressed his head. "No, sweetie."

***

It was after eight in the morning when Kay came back to the waiting room to find Ryan standing by the window looking out over the bleak winter landscape. She paused a moment before she approached him, formulating her words. She placed a hand on his shoulder and he turned around.

"How is he?" he asked.

Kay put her arms around him and clutched him, placing her cheek against his chest. "Just hold me." She let out a deep breath and melted into Ryan.

They stayed that way for several minutes until Kay pulled away, looked up and Ryan, and shook her head, whispering, "They have to do more tests. It may take a week."

"I'm here for you."

***

A week passed, Kay staying with Easton night and day, wearing a surgical mask to minimize him getting infections. Ryan stayed in the waiting room and came into Easton's room to visit, also wearing a mask. Ryan drew smiles on his and Kay's masks to make them look less frightening to three-year-old Easton, Ryan's missing a tooth.

Two doctors wearing masks walked in, one she didn't recognize. She searched their eyes for any sign of hope. "The results of the tests came in. Can we talk in my office?"

She looked at Ryan.

He nodded. "Go ahead. I've got him."

***

Half an hour later, she reappeared. Easton was asleep. So was Ryan in the chair Kay spent the last week in. She paused at the door. Something about her boy and Ryan—she couldn't put her finger on it. She went to Ryan and gently shook him awake, signaling him to follow her.

They sat in the waiting room. She lowered her head and searched for the words she was afraid to say out loud. She let out a deep sigh. "They brought in a specialist. Easton has stage-four leukemia."

"Oh, Kay." Ryan wrapped an arm around her shoulders and she leaned into him.

She shook her head. "His only chance is a bone marrow transplant—and I'm not a match." She trembled as she said the words, "And I promised him."

"Why don't I get tested?"

"Oh, Ryan." Their eyes met, both filled with tears. "That'd be nice, but they think someone with native blood will only be a match."

"Maybe someone from your church or—"

"Just hold me," Kay said and she buried herself in Ryan."

***

The church bulletin prompted a handful of members to get tested over the next few weeks, but no match. Someone passed along the Church's bulletin to an editor at the Big Horn County News. They called Kay for an interview and wrote up an article for the local paper—a last hope.

During the next few weeks, a dozen more people showed up to get tested, again with the same meager results.

***

The loudspeakers in the hospital blared, "Kay Goodtree to the nurses' station. Kay Goodtree to the nurses' station. You have a call."

Kay and Ryan exchanged glances.

Kay patted Easton on the arm and said through her mask, "I'll be right back."

Who'd be calling me?

Kay trudged down the shiny gray linoleum hall, her shoes squeaking all the way to the hub of activity in the middle of the corridor.

A nurse pointed to a phone on the counter. "Line two," she said.

Kay picked up the receiver and punched the blinking light for line two. "This is Kay Goodtree."

"Finally," a voice Kay never thought she'd hear from again said, "I found you."

25

Kay paused in the doorway to Easton's room, and noticing him asleep, slumped into the doorframe. She let out a deep sigh and Ryan turned towards her whispering, "What's the matter?"

Kay bent over and held her gut as if she'd been punched. She weakly waved him over and stepped into the hallway, leaning against a wall.

Ryan joined her, concern all over his face. "You're white as a ghost. You alright?" Ryan placed a hand on her shoulder.

Kay moaned, "She's here."

"Who?"

"Linda, my dead husband's mother. She threatened to..." her voice faded and she shook her head.

"What can she do?"

"Anything and everything," Kay answered. She stood up straight. "She's wealthy, Ryan. Not Bill Gates wealthy, but up there. I took Easton away from her because she was suffocating us, invading every aspect of our lives, reminding me of Logan—my dead husband." She looked into Ryan's eyes. "I left in the middle of the night without a trace—just a note asking her not to look for me."

"But she has—been looking for you."

"Yes."

"Is Kay your real name?"

Kay blushed with shame and lowered her head. "No. It's Kennedy. Kennedy Young." She buried her face in her hands and mumbled, "I don't know what to do."

Ryan wrapped his arms around her and whispered, "We'll figure out something."

***

Kennedy heard Linda Young before she saw her. "I demand to see my grandson now!" her voice carried down the hospital corridor.

Kennedy and Ryan peeked out Easton's door and noticed Linda with an entourage of three men, two in suits. Linda, as always, was dressed to intimidate with her perfect hair, expensive jewels, and her fifty-five-year-old fake-tanned Pilates body.

Linda spotted Kennedy. "There you are!" Linda started down the hall but a hospital security man blocked her way.

Linda's bodyguard stepped in and shoved the security man who barked into his shoulder mic, "Code gray, second floor nurses' station, code gray."

The bodyguard paused for a second, then continued to push the security man aside.

"STOP!" The head nurse, a 40ish, feisty five feet tall with flaming red hair, stormed into the mix with her arms up and halted everything. "What the hell are you doing on my floor?"

"I've come to see my grandson," Linda declared, trying to stare down the nurse.

The head nurse put her hands on her hips and returned a glare. "Not on my watch—not this way."

Additional hospital security men arrived and surrounded Linda and her cohorts.

"I have my rights." She pointed to a man in a suit next to her carrying a briefcase. "This is my lawyer, Mr. Thomas Gimball. No doubt you've heard of him. You do not want to feel the wrath he can bring on you and your Crow-Northern Cheyenne Hospital."

"I don't care if he's the Pope himself, no one, and I mean no one, goes down my hallway without screening and proper precautions. If you take one more step, I'll have you arrested—and enjoy doing it. You will not put my patients in danger."

The third gentleman with Linda stepped forward before Linda could speak. "I'm Dr. Bernard Langston. I specialize in pediatric oncology and fully understand and appreciate your precautions. Where can Mrs. Young acquire the necessary garb to visit her grandson?"

The head nurse looked him up and down, then nodded. "That's more like it. Right this way."

***

Doctor Moore's office was packed—Kennedy sat in a chair across from his desk, Linda in another, with her entourage standing behind her. Easton's status and treatment options had been discussed and debated for hours.

Dr. Langston snapped shut Easton's chart and handed it to Dr. Moore. "The way I see it, Dr. Moore, as advanced as the cancer is, the only chance you have to save Easton is a bone marrow transplant—and the match has to be perfect. No matter what, the boy needs to stay here. Moving him's out of the question." He turned to Kennedy. "You've had, what, a couple dozen tests run with no match. Since you weren't a match, how about Linda? Sometimes maternal grandmothers are perfect."

Linda winced. "Well, I don't know about that…" her words faded and she winced.

Dr. Langston reached out to her shoulder. "It's a fairly simple procedure."

Kennedy squirmed in her chair. "Maybe you're too, well, old."

Linda shot her a glare. "No, I'm not. Test me."

***

Every time Kennedy looked around, there was Ryan—by Easton's bed, getting her something, or sleeping in the waiting room.

Ryan, you're something special.

Sometimes she'd sneak down the corridor to Easton's room and watch the two of them as Ryan read to him, or they watched cartoons, or chatted about things a three-year-old was curious about. Ryan had a patience about him that was … she couldn't find the words to describe it.

When Easton fell into a deep sleep, Kennedy and Ryan snuck down to the cafeteria to get a bite to eat. Kennedy sat across from Ryan at one of the orange and gray tables, sniffed the air, and smiled. "They cooked fish tonight."

"Sure did." Ryan rolled his coffee mug between his hands.

Kennedy cleared her throat. "You've been here over three weeks now. I feel kinda guilty with, you know, taking up so much of your time."

He cocked his head. "Time means nothing to me right now. But to your son, it means everything. Easton's clock is ticking. I want to—no, I need to—make every minute count. He's special in a way I can't explain."

Kennedy nodded and drew in a deep breath. "I've got to ask you something ... is it only Easton you're interested in, or..." she wasn't brave enough to say the words.

Ryan reached across the table and took Kennedy's hands, looking into her dark eyes framed by high cheek bones and long black hair. "You, too."

Kennedy felt her cheeks flush, and in Ryan's blue eyes and blond hair could see what Easton might look like if he lived 20 more years.

If he lives.

Ryan continued, "The raven brought me to you, but you have more important things going on. Your boy needs you and I feel he needs me. If we can get past this disease, I'd like to see what that bird had in mind for us." He offered Kennedy a brave smile.

She gave his hands a quick squeeze. "So would I."

***

It took a week for Linda's results to come in and she flew back from La Jolla, finding no hotels in Montana to her liking.

Dr. Moore sat in his chair, his graying hair over his ears—a man too busy to care for himself. He read the report aloud in his office with only Linda and Kennedy in attendance, finishing with, "What's unusual is that we didn't even find a few of your markers, even in your DNA, that aligned with Easton. No match whatsoever, Mrs. Young."

Linda let out a sigh, like she was relieved the results came back negative. "Now what?"

Kennedy sat forward in her chair. "Yes, what do we do now?"

"Broaden our search for possible donors." Dr. Moore grimaced. "We don't have much time and it'll be costly."

"I can—" Kennedy started.

Linda cut her off. "Money's not a problem, not when my grandson's life depends on it."

***

Dr. Moore gave Easton a few transfusions of high-count white blood to stave off infection and buy them some needed time. Linda got her PR machine working, running ads in major newspapers and contacting blood banks across the nation.

Three weeks later, Linda flew up for another meeting with Kennedy and Dr. Moore—and to see Easton.

Before they went into the doctor's office, Linda took Kennedy aside. "You know, it's all your fault. You, running away like you did. The stress, and god knows what kind of diseases you exposed that boy to, that's what made him sick. You should be ashamed of yourself."

Tears filled Kennedy's eyes. "You don't have to remind me. I've felt that way ever since he came to the hospital."

"Leaving me, his grandmother, the way you did. We had a wonderful little life going in La Jolla. It wasn't really so bad, was it?"

Kennedy lowered her head and shook it.

Linda took Kennedy's hand and patted it. "Come now, Dear. Let's find out what the doctor plans to do next."

They walked into his office, surprised to find Dr. Moore standing by the window humming. Linda had to stomp her feet to get him to notice they arrived.

He spun around. "Sorry, sorry. Ladies, please have a seat." He gestured with his hand, and instead of sitting behind his desk, rolled his chair over to sit next to them. He leaned forward and took off his glasses, hope in his eyes. "I have some good news for you."

"A match?" Linda asked.

He nodded his head.

"I told you I'd find one," Linda said gloating.

Kennedy ignored her. "Who is it?"

He studied her as if she wasn't ready to hear the news. "You know him. His DNA and HLA, that's human leukocyte antigens, they're a match."

"Who?" Kennedy asked.

"Ryan Turner."

Kennedy's mouth dropped. "My Ryan?"

"Yes, the young man who's been helping you."

Linda snorted. "Him? It can't be."

"Ryan insisted we test him and paid for it himself. He's a perfect match." The doctor's eyebrows raised and he tilted his head. "If I didn't know better, I'd say he and Easton were related somehow."

"Ha!" Linda said. "There must be a mistake. Right, Kennedy?"

Kennedy looked down at her hands—hands Ryan held dozens of times in the past few weeks. Then there was the way he held and comforted her. The way he was with Easton. She stared out the window, shook her head, and whispered, "No, it couldn't be." A chill ran through her.

The voice of Miss Betty Old Horn spoke to Kennedy as if coming from a lost dream.

The raven—it was me, leading Ryan to you.

26

Kennedy and Ryan stood on opposite sides of Easton's bed with their masks on. To keep it light, Ryan drew a fake smile on his mask with a tooth missing. The sun's last rays peeked through the window blinds.

"Tomorrow, Ryan's going to share his blood with you, Easton," Kennedy said as she bent down and brushed the blond hair from his forehead.

Easton looked to Ryan. "Will it hurt you?"

"No. We'll both be asleep. Isn't that cool?" Ryan asked, his eyes squinting from a smile.

Easton grinned and nodded his head.

"It should make you better. No more dizzy spells." Kennedy's eyes filled with hope, something she hadn't felt in almost two months. "You need to get some rest now, okay?"

He nodded. Kennedy reached up and turned off the light.

"See you in the morning," Ryan whispered.

"Me too," Kennedy added and kissed Easton's forehead.

Ryan and Kennedy stayed with Easton until his even deep breaths told them he was asleep. They tiptoed out of his room.

Kennedy walked with Ryan to his room where he'd spend the night in prep for his surgery. They went in, sat on the edge of his bed, and took off their masks.

She reached over and took his hand. "I bet you never thought driving through Montana would turn out like this, did you?"

"No. But I'm so glad I did." Ryan squeezed her hand. "There's something you need to know about me." He paused not knowing how to tell her. "After my parents' murder, and after my time in the Marines, I tried to kill the man who murdered my parents."

Kennedy let go of Ryan's hand and sat back. "My god. What happened?"

"He was in my rifle sights on the courtroom steps, when the raven stopped me."

"The raven again?"

"Yes."

"My grandmother, Miss Betty Old Horn—she spoke to me after the doctor told me you were Easton's match. She said she was the raven who brought you to me." She turned on the bed towards Ryan. "And I believe it."

"Hopefully my marrow will cure Easton. That's all the matters."

Kennedy stood. "Well, I'm glad you're in our lives—and not just because you're the perfect donor." She patted his hand. "You better get some rest. You've got a long day ahead of you."

When Kennedy exited Ryan's room, there was Dr. Moore waiting for her with an envelope in his hand.

More for me to sign?

He smiled. "You should have this," he said as he handed her the paper. "It's Ryan's DNA results."

Kennedy opened the enveloped and pulled out a sheet of paper. She stared at it—a 99.9997% match.

"Results like this can only come from a parent."

Miss Betty Old Horn's voice came to Kennedy again.

It is him.

***

While Easton and Ryan were in surgery, Kennedy and Linda held their own kind of vigil in the waiting room—sitting kitty-corner from each other, Linda buried in a Cosmo magazine, Kennedy silently praying with her head bowed.

After half an hour, Kennedy got up. "I'm going to make a few phone calls. I'll be back."

Linda scowled. "What? And leave me here?"

Kennedy sighed. "It'll just be a few minutes."

"What if something happens when you're gone?"

"They'll page me."

With that, Kennedy headed out the door, ignoring Linda's harrumphs.

***

"And you say the donor was from Michigan. Can you be more precise?" Kennedy asked.

"We can't tell you the name. The donor didn't want it known," the voice on the phone said.

"Well, can you at least give me the city and the date?" Kennedy stood in a phone booth in the lobby of the hospital, a pen in her trembling hand hovering above a sheet of paper.

"Just a moment, please."

Kennedy slumped down to the seat and barely listened to the on-hold music the fertility clinic played—an instrumental version of the song *You're Beautiful*. There was a click.

"This is all we can tell you, Mrs. Young. The donor made his deposit during the month of October 2003, and it was made in Kalamazoo." She paused. "I hope that helps."

Kennedy dropped the pen and paper.

It is you.

She couldn't think or talk.

"Mrs. Young, are you still there?"

"Uh, yes. Thank you." After she hung up, Miss Betty Old Horn's words swirled in her head along with every moment she spent with Ryan. The way the raven guided Ryan to her from around the world, the gentle and loving way he was with Easton … how he was with her, so kind and...

She shuddered, tears rolling down her face as a mixture of excitement and awe flooded her.

***

Kennedy entered the waiting room on a cloud and stopped when she found Linda whispering to her lawyer in a corner. She cautiously interrupted, "What's he doing here?"

Linda and Mr. Gimball turned to her then looked to each other. Linda nodded to him and he stood, approaching Kennedy with his hand ready to guide her out of the room.

"May I speak with you—privately?" he asked, his starched white monogrammed shirt, red silk tie, and four-thousand-dollar gray suit bolstering his authority.

Kennedy looked around him to Linda. "What's going on?"

A stoic Linda answered, "What's best for everyone—especially my grandson."

Mr. Gimball ushered Kennedy out of the waiting room and down the hall. He opened a door. "Right in here."

Kennedy entered a stark, private room, no doubt used for discussions between social workers and parents, or doctors and anxious relatives—all in the midst of life and death situations.

Kennedy took a seat on a padded beige chair—in fact, everything in the room was decorated in different shades of beige, from the carpet, to the walls, to the furniture.

"What's this all about?" Kennedy asked sitting up straight, a rigid resolve taking hold of her.

He presented himself well, perfectly trimmed graying hair, designer reading glasses, white shark teeth, tanned, and fit.

She must pay you a lot.

"I'm here at the request of Linda—Mrs. Young." He reached in his briefcase and pulled out an envelope with Kennedy's name on it and set it on the table. "Mrs. Young is invoking the clause in your pre-birth agreement. Should a financial burden impede your ability to properly care for Easton, she is allowed to take possession of the child."

He pushed the envelope across the table to a stunned Kennedy. "That's five million dollars—tax free."

Kennedy stared at the envelope, then looked at the lawyer with the eyes of a mother protecting her child from a wild dog. She pushed the envelope back and snarled, "You can tell Linda to go to hell. Easton's staying with me."

"Look," Mr. Gimball said, turning on kind and understanding eyes, "Easton's hospital stay and surgery is going to cost over half a million dollars. Without insurance—"

Kennedy cut him off. "I'll pay it."

"How are you going to do that?"

"It'll take everything I've got, but I'll manage." Kennedy nodded with a finality, realizing her dreams for Easton's financial future were gone.

Mr. Gimball's demeanor shifted from kindly advice to attack dog. He slid his glasses down his nose and squinted at her. "Understand this, you'll spend another million dollars or more in court defending the lawsuits Mrs. Young will bring. Do you want that kind of life for you and your son?"

Kennedy stared at him and shook her head. Then a smile spread across her face. She remained that way for several uncomfortable moments.

Mr. Gimball cleared his throat and asked, "What's so amusing?"

"This—this whole charade. Linda won't want a thing to do with Easton or me. In fact, your contract is void."

Mr. Gimball leaned forward and jutted out his jaw. "And why is that?"

Kennedy leaned into him, inches away from his face and whispered. "Because Easton's not her grandchild."

Mr. Gimball pulled back and gulped. "What? You're saying you had an affair?"

"No. I'm saying Logan was sterile and I had to do something—because he raped me nearly every day. I got pregnant by a sperm donor." She said the next words slowly, as

227

if Mr. Gimball were a two-year-old. "Easton is not Logan's son. He's not Linda's grandson."

"Well then, if you can prove that and—"

Kennedy cut him. "I can do more than that." She reached into her purse and slid an envelope to him. "His biological father is in surgery right now and he's going to give his life-saving bone marrow to Easton."

For a man so used to confrontation and ready to deal with any situation, Mr. Gimball's mouth hung open as he worked to analyze all the legal implications as he extracted the lab report from the envelope.

Kennedy smiled. "That's right. And as I recall, the entire agreement is based on the fact that Easton is her blood relative."

Mr. Gimball stood. "I'll have to talk to Mrs. Young about this."

"You do that."

Mr. Gimball stood, picked up both envelopes, and headed for the door—but not before he took one last look at Kennedy, her teeth clenched. He swung the door open and left the room.

Kennedy stayed in the small meeting room, not wanting to hear the words of hate Linda would spew. A watercolor on the wall caught her attention and she stood and moved to it to get a closer look. A cart filled with hay rolled up a rise pulled by a small chestnut horse. Sun tried to break through stormy skies, a lone dark bird circling overhead. Next to the man driving the cart was a woman in peasant clothes—and between them was a small child. Kennedy's heart swelled with hope.

Thank you, Miss Betty.

***

By the time Kennedy returned to the waiting room, Linda and her lawyer were gone, but the sour odor of Linda's anger and disappointment still lingered in the air.

Dr. Morris peeked in and lowered his surgical mask, a smile on his face. "Kennedy?"

She spun around with anxious eyes.

"You can relax. Ryan's procedure went well." He looked around. "Where's Linda, uh, Mrs. Young?"

Kennedy beamed. "She's gone."

"Well, I've got to get back to Easton to finish the transplant. Should be done in a couple of hours. Ryan's in recovery now if you want to see him." He smiled, a knowing look on his face.

"I will."

***

Kennedy was there when Ryan woke, his groggy eyes trying to focus on her warm smile. She placed a loving hand on his face and kept it there.

"How'd it go?" he mumbled.

"Fine. The doctor said just fine."

"Good," he said, his eyes fluttering, mumbling softly as he drifted back to sleep.

Kennedy remained standing by his bed holding his hand until he awoke fifteen minutes later.

"You again," he grinned, more alert.

Her eyes sparkled. "Yes, me again." She squeezed his hand.

"How's Easton?"

"Still in surgery. It's only been an hour."

"When can we see him?"

"As soon as possible." Kennedy took a deep breath. "Ryan, you're Easton's father. I called the clinic. You donated sperm at a clinic in Kalamazoo four years ago, didn't you?"

"Yeah…"

"It has to be, the DNA match speaks for itself."

Ryan blinked his eyes clear and tried to scoot up in bed, wincing from the discomfort. "Can I really be his father?"

"You are." She gulped. "The hair. The blue eyes. The raven that brought you here."

***

Two weeks later, Dr. Moore proclaimed Easton well enough to go home, but precautions against infection must be taken to extremes. That meant sterilizing her home, wearing masks at all times, no exposure to anyone with even a sniffle, no other children, hand sanitizers, and healthy non-cancer-feeding foods.

Ryan spent all his time at Kennedy's home, playing with Easton, and sharing popcorn while watching old movies after Easton went to bed. Sometimes they fell asleep on her sofa with just the fireplace to keep them company, but Ryan always returned to his hotel room.

There was a quiet understanding between them—Easton's health came first. If something were to work out between them, that would come later after Easton was out of danger. They held hands and cuddled but never kissed—Kennedy unsure and not ready to trust a man again. The attraction and pull was there though, and Miss Betty Old Horn's words kept repeating in Kennedy's heart.

The raven was me, leading Ryan to you.

***

Three weeks passed when Easton, Kennedy, and Ryan, all wearing masks with smiles drawn on them, were back in Dr. Moore's office for a checkup. Dr. Moore, wearing a mask as well, scanned the lab results, letting out an occasional "hmm" and "ahh" between wrinkled and softening eyebrows. He let out a long sigh and looked up, nodding his head.

"Easton's T-cells and white blood counts are way up—to normal levels."

"What does that mean," Kennedy asked, sitting up and leaning forward.

Dr. Moore removed his mask. "You can take off your masks now—all of you," he answered. "Easton's antibodies are doing their job getting rid of the cancer." He looked down at Easton's file. "Let's schedule a follow-up a month from now, on the twenty-fourth. Then, if that's clear, we'll do another checkup in three months. Sound good?"

Kennedy removed her mask and her voice cracked. "Good? It's—it's wonderful." She turned to Easton and removed his mask. "Your daddy's blood made you better."

She locked eyes with Ryan as he took off his mask, a grin on his flushed face.

Easton looked up at his mother, then Ryan. "My daddy?" he asked beaming.

Ryan's eyes glistened. "My boy."

***

On the way home, they stopped by the Dairy Queen in Hardin to celebrate, their first public outing in three months. Ryan sat on one side of the booth, Easton and Kennedy on the other. Easton shoveled dripping spoonfuls of strawberry ice cream in his mouth, some getting on his face and shirt—no one cared.

Ryan and Kennedy stole glances at Easton and then each other. Their hands reached across the table and touched, but it was different this time.

After they got back to her place, Ryan put on a song mix, they made dinner, played with Easton, and put him to bed.

Kennedy and Ryan ended up on the sofa as usual. A small fire was accompanied by wine, their way of celebrating. Ryan raised his glass and so did Kennedy.

"To our little man—he's really something," Ryan said.

They clinked glasses.

"To us," Kennedy whispered and stared into Ryan's blue eyes and they took sips.

Etta James' song *At Last* was on in the background and Ryan mumbled along to the last words.

"…You are mine, at last."

That was the final song on the mix. The only sounds remaining in the room were the crackle of the fire and their heavy breaths. Kennedy set her wine glass down, took Ryan's face in her hands, and kissed him. It was a soft kiss, filled with a lifetime of longing for the tenderness she desired. Kennedy snuggled into Ryan and let out a deep sigh.

"I couldn't kiss you before. I wanted to, but…" her voice trailed off.

Ryan set down his glass and took her gently by the shoulders so that their eyes met. "The raven, your grandmother, she watched over me—brought me back from the dead twice and kept me from throwing my life away—the life I want to spend with you."

He kissed her with the patience and passion of a lover who had the rest of his life to share a million more kisses.

End

Made in the USA
San Bernardino,
CA